tales from scottish lairds

JARROLD

Castles and Houses open to the Public

In addition to most of the properties featured in this book, many other Scottish castles and mansions are open to the public. Some are in the care of the National Trust for Scotland, and details of such properties are available from the Trust at 5 Charlotte Square, Edinburgh EH2 4DU; tel: (0131) 226 5922. Others are maintained by Historic Scotland, 20 Brandon Street, Edinburgh EH3 5RA; tel: (0131) 244 3099/3144, or by local civil authorities or preservation trusts. Many are still family homes, but are open at certain times to enable the public to enjoy their beauty and atmosphere. The visitor should enquire at local tourist information offices or consult the annual publication *Historic Houses, Castles and Gardens* (produced by British Leisure Publications, East Grinstead) for details of properties in the area.

While every effort has been made to give accurate dates and times of opening, the publishers cannot be held responsible for any errors, changes or omissions which may occur, and the prospective visitor is advised to check opening times with the local tourist information office, castle or house, before planning a visit.

Acknowledgements

The publishers would like to thank all those who helped in the creation of this book by writing a story or providing information. Thanks are especially due to Mrs Elisabeth Fraser, who selected and liaised with those castle and houses appearing in the book, and to the late Lord Maclean, KT, GCVO, KBE, who provided the Foreword.

ISBN 0-7117-0814-2

© Jarrold Publications 1985
Revised reprint 1995
Jarrold Publications, Norwich
Printed in Great Britain. 3/95

contents

foreword

By the late Lord Maclean, KT, GCVO, KBE
27th Chief of Clan Maclean

The visitor to Scotland's many historic Castles and Mansions must often have wondered about the ancestors of the present occupants – the life they led, the clan feuds and warfare, the battles between the Scots and the English before the Union of the two countries.

The visitor may also have felt, while walking through ancient rooms and up and down twisting turret stairs, some sensation of things unseen, or inexplicable fears, or suddenly felt cold on a hot summer's day. The guide, when questioned, may speak of a haunted room or ghostly apparition but usually knows few details.

Now, in this collection of stories, some told by the Chiefs or Chieftains themselves, and all handed down in their families through the centuries, visitors will discover a vivid picture of life in more warlike times. The castles which today are comfortable family homes were once strong defences against attack by neighbouring clans. This warlike tradition is blended with a strong belief in the powers of the supernatural – in fairies, ghostly armies and events which warn of death. These beliefs are not always to be scoffed at, as many previous sceptics have discovered when confronted with some thing or noise which they cannot explain. Even in those mansions which do not have such a long history, customs have changed greatly since the beginning of this century. The vast armies of menservants and maidservants once necessary for the smooth running of the establishments are now no longer to be found, but they have left their own mark and are often fondly remembered in family anecdotes.

It is hoped that, as a result of reading these tales, the visitor to each house or castle included here will feel a greater understanding of the part it played in Scotland's history; or, when suddenly sensing an unseen presence in some old chamber, will now know the identity of his invisible companion.

Maclean
of Duart + Morvern.

Duart Castle

Duart Castle, ancient seat of the chiefs of the Macleans, is built strategically on the east coast of the Isle of Mull, commanding the eastern entrance to the Sound of Mull. The first recorded mention of the castle is in 1390; the keep was probably constructed about this time by Lachlan Lubanach Maclean, Chief of the clan. However, the massive curtain-walls, ten feet thick on the landward side, and thirty feet high, are earlier, probably dating from the thirteenth century. A deep ditch cut into the solid rock is an additional protection beyond the landward walls. The protection of the sea on the other side meant that here the walls needed to be less thick, only six to eight feet generally.

The Macleans lived in the castle for the next 300 years. During the Civil Wars of the seventeenth century, they supported the Stuart kings, and were later staunch Jacobites. However, they incurred heavy debts, during the Civil Wars, which were bought up by the Campbells. After a number of years, and when the Jacobites were finally defeated, the Campbells managed eventually to lay waste to Duart and ruin the family fortunes.

It was only in 1911 that Colonel Sir Fitzroy Maclean was able to buy back the castle ruin and part of the surrounding peninsular lands. He carried out a programme of extensive restoration and made it once again the seat of the Chief of the Clan Maclean.

Opening times:
May–September
Daily 10.30–18.00
Tel: (01680) 812309

9

Over the centuries, Duart has been the focal point for many exciting or strange happenings.

Violence seems to have been an accepted way of life in those far-off times, and there was a succession of inter-clan feuds and, sometimes, even family feuds. In one such struggle, Hector Mor Maclean of Duart supported Iain the Toothless Maclaine of Lochbuie against a rising led by Iain's only son, Eachuin of the Little Head. Eachuin was killed but his ghost, 'The Headless Horseman', is still said to appear on his phantom steed, terrifying anyone unfortunate enough to glimpse him, whenever the death of a chief of the Maclaines of Lochbuie is imminent. After the rising had been quashed, Hector Mor imprisoned Iain the Toothless on a secluded island. No woman was to be permitted near this island, so that there would be no chance of Iain producing a son and heir. However, Hector made the mistake of allowing Iain one maidservant who, being deformed and extremely unattractive, was presumed by Hector to present no threat as the potential mother of an heir. All the same, Iain proved that desperation overcomes attraction, and she bore him a son, fittingly named Murdoch the Stunted, who eventually made his way to Mull, after many adventures, where he carried on the succession of the Maclaines of Lochbuie.

Perhaps the most ruthless tale of Duart concerns the sixteenth-century Chief, Lachlan Cattanach Maclean. Because it seemed advisable for the Macleans to form an alliance with the powerful Campbells of Argyll, he married Lady Catherine Campbell, the sister of Argyll. However, he soon grew bored with her, especially as she did not provide him with any children. In retaliation for this barrenness, Lachlan stranded poor Catherine on a rock which he knew would be covered by the incoming tide, and left her to drown. To this day, the rock is known as 'The Lady Rock', and it can still be seen from Duart when the tide is low. Fortunately for the Lady Catherine, some passing fishermen noticed her predicament, rescued her and took her back to her brother.

However, the outcome was not so good for her cruel and unfeeling husband. Eagerly anticipating her death, he had (in broken tones) reported the event to the Earl of Argyll. Naturally, the Earl was incensed when his sister was returned to him and he learnt what had really happened. Revenge was not long in coming, for in 1523 the Thane of Cawdor, another of Catherine's brothers, caught up with Lachlan Maclean in Edinburgh and 'dirked him in bed'.

During the sixteenth century, Scotland was linked with Ireland by a trade-route, and marriages were arranged to strengthen the link. Catherine Maclean, the sister of Duart and the widow of Argyll, married The O'Donnell, ruler of Tirconail, but was then captured by The O'Neill, ruler of Tyrone, who used her as his mistress. She was 'chained by day to a little boy, and only released to amuse her master's drunken leisure', a cruel fate for a lady who was unusually well educated for her day, having some knowledge of Latin, and speaking French and Italian.

Control of the trade-routes to Ireland led to a bitter feud between the Macleans and the Macdonalds. The chief of Clan Maclean at this time was Sir Lachlan Mor Maclean, one of the most distinguished of all the chiefs, and with a blood-stained history behind him. Lachlan only came into his inheritance after his followers had captured the Tutor of Duart by invading the castle in the middle of the night, and had beheaded him. One of his most shocking acts took place at the celebration of his own mother's remarriage. Sir Lachlan burst into the wedding-feast, murdered eighteen of the guests and imprisoned and tortured the bridegroom (who was a Clan Donald chieftain).

In the best dramatic tradition, Sir Lachlan's death in 1598 was foretold by the appearance of a fiery comet. In a way, he could be said to have brought his death upon himself, because sometime earlier he had been warned that great misfortune would follow if he ever sailed his galleys anti-clockwise round the little island of Eilean Armalaig in Loch Spelve. Sir Lachlan ignored the warning and disaster overtook him soon afterwards at the Battle of Traigh Ghruineard on Islay, when he was killed by a hunchbacked dwarf whom he had once scorned. Sir Lachlan's sons were quick to avenge their father's murder, embarking on a vicious massacre which extended over three horror-filled days. But with Lachlan's death the clan had lost one of its greatest leaders and from this point on the fortunes of the clan went steadily downhill, to be revived only in the present century.

scone palace

Scone Palace overlooks the Tay and the city of Perth, known as the 'Fair City'. The chroniclers of Scone's past tell of Druids, of Romans tramping through the park, and give fantastic glimpses of the kings of old and of king-making: of the high kings of the Picts in their kingdom of Scone; then later of the kings of Scots in the royal city of Scone; of the legendary kings, Macbeth and Robert the Bruce, being made King here; of the great treasure of Scone – its sacred stone, known as the 'Stone of Scone'. As well as being the Coronation site, and the capital of Scotland, Scone had also Scotland's first Parliaments.

Scone was, for a thousand years, successively the site of the monastery of the Culdees, then a priory and abbey of Augustinian Canons. The Abbey of Scone and Bishop's House were sacked and burnt in 1559, by a wild mob who had been greatly inflamed by John Knox's sermon in Perth. The existing palace, built in 1581, gained its present appearance when, in 1802–04, it was extensively Gothicised, adapted and enlarged by the architect William Atkinson. His style was well suited to Scone's monastic past. Today the palace is entered by the east door in front of which lie, unseen, the unmarked graves of shallowly buried bodies from hundreds of years past.

The story which follows was written by the Countess of Mansfield.

Opening times:
Early April – early October; other dates by appointment
Mon–Sat 09.30–17.00, Sun (July–August from 10.00) 13.30–17.00
Tel: (01738) 552300; Fax: (01738) 552588

Scone is the home of the eighth Earl of Mansfield and his wife and family of two sons and a daughter. The family name is Murray, whose origins go back no little time. Freskin (de Moravia), roving Flemish nobleman with an equally roving eye, married Macbeth's daughter and started a long line of Murrays from which Lord Mansfield is descended through the then Earls of Atholl.

The lands and the Palace of Scone passed in 1603 to David Murray, who was later made Lord Stormont. He became a highly successful fellow, his career having been given a boost when one day he, and his friends and retainers, were returning from a family wedding and rode by the Earl of Gowrie's town house in Perth. When they heard King James VI of Scotland shouting desperately from a tower, David Murray and his group rushed, with drawn swords, to save the King, whose life was being threatened by one of the Gowrie family. The King was so grateful for being saved that he gave David Murray the Earl of Gowrie's Lands of Scone, and created him Lord Scone. David had indeed 'made good'. He became Ceremonial Cup-Bearer to the King and his Master of the Horse; he was also Comptroller of Scotland and, later, Captain of the King's Guard. In 1621 he was advanced to be Viscount of Stormont. It was soon after this that he built a little church on the Moot Hill.

Other Murrays before David, and the Murrays right up to the present day, always enjoyed being in the thick of things, the present Earl being no exception. This branch of the Murrays has always produced great patriots, successful and nice, a combination not often found in life! That a Murray will always be willing to talk things out, where others would prefer a quicker conclusion by drawing their swords, was suggested by their neighbours, in the old Litany:

> From the greed of the Campbells
> From the ire of the Drummonds
> From the pride of the Grahams, and
> From the wind of the Murrays,
> Good Lord, deliver us!

This 'wind of the Murrays' refers, of course, to a charming and persuasive eloquence with which this line of Murrays has been blessed.

Another, later, Viscount Stormont helped at the coronation at Scone of King Charles II. It took place nine years before Charles's Restoration in London in 1660. This Coronation took place on New Year's Day 1651 and was the only purely Presbyterian coronation. The day was bitterly cold and the tiny church on the Moot Hill was crammed, with many more poor wretches shivering outside, while two very boring orations were made. The Moderator of the General Assembly gave a sermon lasting an hour and a half and Lord Lyon King of Arms gave a fascinating, for some, recitation of Charles's family tree going back to Fergus, King of Scots, in 490, which took another hour and a half! This icy and prolonged ceremony was the last coronation ever to be performed in Scotland; it is not recorded how many people got pneumonia as a result!

The family remained in the thick of Scottish politics. Bonnie Prince Charlie was received at Scone as he had been brought up by a brother of the sixth Viscount Stormont. Another brother – William Murray – became the greatest lawyer of all time and was created first Earl of Mansfield. One of ten children, when small he had run barefoot in the streets of Perth where the then impoverished family had a town house. William rose to become a most powerful and wealthy man. He was Lord Chief Justice for the still-record period of thirty-two years, having been successively Solicitor-General, Attorney-General and Lord Chief Justice. Another record he achieved was to have been the only man twice Lord Chief Justice and Chancellor of the Exchequer at the same time. William Murray, Earl of Mansfield, personified the well-known 'wind of the Murrays' and was known as 'silver-tongued Murray'. This brilliant man was kindly and humane, and not only did he create the commercial law of Britain and of the United States of America, but he laid down that slavery was 'odious' and that once any man set foot in Britain, he was free. He thus struck the first real blow against the Slave Trade. On his death, a huge monument was erected in Westminster Abbey to the memory and honour of his name. It is there to this day and stands in the middle of the west aisle of the north transept of the abbey.

This unusually gifted man was succeeded by his nephew, David, seventh Viscount Stormont and second Earl of Mansfield, who was also a highly intelligent and erudite fellow. He was Britain's Envoy to Dresden in 1756, and then Envoy-Extraordinary to Vienna, where he became a friend of the Empress Maria Theresa. Later, he was made Ambassador to the Court of Louis XVI at Versailles, where he charmed both the King and his pretty wife, Queen Marie-Antoinette. The third Earl made the greatest changes at Scone with his Gothicisation in 1802. A few years later he made a take-over bid for the old village of Scone, offering the inhabitants such generous terms to move to a new village placed further from the palace, that they found it impossible to refuse.

The fourth Earl, who was also blessed with the 'wind of the Murrays', entertained Queen Victoria and Prince Albert in 1842, when the Long Gallery floor was used as an iceless rink in order to give the Queen a Curling lesson.

The next two Earls were both brave and bemedalled soldiers. The sixth Earl married the daughter of Sir Malcolm MacGregor of MacGregor, Chief of the Clan MacGregor – 'The Children of the Mist' – by whose mother, a McDonnell, the present Lord Mansfield descends from Red Hugh O'Neill, the last native King of Ulster.

The Stone of Scone
Just in front of the Palace of Scone is a large mound, the Moot Hill, which abounds with glittering legends. Not only is this the site of Scotland's early and first recorded Parliaments, but it is also the site of the coronations of Scotland's early medieval kings.

The story of the Stone of Scone begins with King Droston, the High King of the Picts, ruling from Scone, which had been the Picts' capital for some hundreds of years. Kenneth MacAlpine, a determined Scot, but whose mother was a Pictish Princess, arrived in the capital and asked King Droston and his nobles to a banquet. When his guests had enjoyed plenty of food, and, of course, drink, Kenneth and his men 'drew out the bolts, which held up the boards, and the Picts fell into the hollows of the benches on which they were sitting, so that they could not get up, and the Scots immediately

17

slaughtered them all, tumbled together everywhere and taken suddenly and unexpectedly'. With this most successful, if brutal, 'take-over bid' Kenneth McAlpine made himself King of Scots, ruling from his capital of Scone. He brought the Stone of Destiny to Scone and it remained here for 500 years.

This mystical stone (surely the most famous lump of stone in the world) made many Scottish kings at Scone, including Macbeth. But now we come to a 700-year-old mystery. The English King Edward came to Scone with his troops in 1296 and demanded the Stone of Scone, taking it to London where it has made British monarchs for 600 years. BUT, and here the mystery deepens, did the Abbot, guardian of Scotland's most prized treasure, give the invaders the fabled king-making Stone OR did he hand over a forgery, a stone quickly hacked from the burn-side, having hidden the real Stone in an underground chamber? This is the legend passed down among the local shepherds. The truth may never be known.

In the grounds of Scone then, where now are luxuriant rolling lawns, magnificent trees and fancy shrubs, there is a mixture of the peace and beauty of present times, with the strange feeling that the ancient times are being endlessly re-enacted all round.

Inside the great crenellated walls, Scone Palace itself also has an atmosphere of dignified, contented peace. But the distant sounds of children chattering and dogs scampering blend with other, stranger, sounds. People from earlier centuries seem to continue their own ploys, oblivious of us. I will mention but one in-house ghost. He is known as the 'Boring Walker'. He is heard but not seen, and walks down the south passage. When we walk down it, all the floorboards squeak and groan noisily; when he walks down it, which he does very frequently (always going east to west), there is the unmistakable regular pad of his feet but – on a *stone floor*! No squeaking floorboards! Is he a guard, a night-watchman, an ancient insomniac? Sadly, we cannot tell. I used to leap out of bed and peer nervously round the bedroom door but the noise of footsteps always continued unchecked, receding down the passage. He is typical of people from the past at Scone – heard – but not seen!

eilean donan castle

Eilean Donan Castle is romantically placed on a little island in Loch Duich, to the east of Kyle of Lochalsh. Steep hillsides rise all round, and create what must be one of the most beautiful of all Scottish castle settings. Despite the castle's idyllic appearance, it stands at the strategically important meeting-point of three lochs and was built to withstand a long siege. The original castle was built during the reign of Alexander II, in the thirteenth century. After standing for 500 years, it then lay in ruins for another 200 years, until rebuilt and restored to its medieval appearance by Lieutenant-Colonel John MacRae-Gilstrap in 1920–32.

The story which follows was written by Mrs Marigold MacRae.

Conchra Charitable Trust

Opening times:
Easter–September
Daily 10.00–18.00
Tel: (01599) 555202

19

Eilean Donan today belies the violence and terror of earlier centuries, when Norse and Danish adventurers raided along the coast and sailed up the sea-loch called Loch Alsh to Loch Duich. Later, the castle afforded protection during savage clan feuds and warfare. It became the stronghold of the MacRaes, the bodyguard of the Chiefs of Kintail, who were appointed Constables of the castle.

Duncan MacRae was a prominent man in the affairs of Kintail during the middle years of the sixteenth century. It was he who gained great renown for himself by killing Donald Gorm MacDonald of Sleat, a Lord of the Isles, at the siege of Eilean Donan in 1539.

The events leading up to this siege and killing were typical of the violence of those times. Some time previously, Donald Gorm had devastated the lands of MacLeod of Dunvegan, an ally of John of Killin, and had then crossed over to the mainland. There he laid waste the district of Kinlochewe and killed, among others, Miles, the son of Finlay MacRae. John of Killin was naturally much angered by this invasion of his territory, as well as by the raid against his friend and ally MacLeod of Dunvegan. He, therefore, sent his son Kenneth with a large band of followers off to Sleat to attack the MacDonalds.

Donald Gorm at once invaded Kintail with a strong party of men and carried off a great deal of booty. He aggravated matters further by killing Sir Dougal MacKenzie, Priest of Kintail, who lived in Glenshiel. The feuding then continued for some considerable time, with raids being carried out on both sides.

Then Donald Gorm received a message to say that Eilean Donan Castle was very weakly garrisoned. He at once decided to make a lightning raid upon the castle with a number of galleys full of his followers, hoping to take it by surprise. The Constable of the castle at the time was John Dubh Matheson of Fernaig. He had married Sir Dougal MacKenzie's widow and had just succeeded Christopher MacRae as Constable. John Dubh and a watchman were the only people in the castle and they viewed the gathering of galleys with great alarm because it left them with no time to send for reinforcements from the mainland before the enemy would be upon them.

21

By a lucky chance, Duncan MacRae was passing by on his way from Loch Alsh and hearing cries of alarm he made for the castle as fast as he could and arrived before the enemy. As the MacDonalds had just killed his uncle, Miles MacRae, he was thirsting for revenge. Taking his stand at the postern gate of the tower he killed several members of the crew of the first galley as they landed. Then, with the enemy crowding in on him in increasing numbers, he retreated into the tower and, barricading the gate behind him, joined the Constable and the watchman in defending the castle.

Donald Gorm immediately began a furious battering of the gate, but the gallant three had secured it so strongly with iron bars and they harassed the besiegers so much by throwing stones at them that he had to withdraw his men. Both sides now began to use their bows, and arrows were soon thick in the air. The MacDonalds, who had already lost many of their men, aimed at the embrasures and managed to hit the Constable, killing him. Duncan was now left alone with the watchman and his last arrow to defend the castle. He decided to keep the arrow for a really favourable opportunity.

Meanwhile, the masts of some of the galleys were taken down, on the orders of Donald Gorm, to make a battering-ram. Donald Gorm then moved round the castle, looking for the weakest and most suitable point of attack. Duncan seized the opportunity and, taking aim, struck him on the foot. The arrow was barbed and, in pulling it out, a main artery was severed. Every possible effort was made to stop the bleeding, but to no avail. The wounded Chief was taken by his men to a reef some distance from the castle, where he died. This disaster marked the end of the attempt on the castle.

It was not until 200 years later that the castle had to withstand another attack of such ferocity. In 1719, during the first Jacobite Rising, a Spanish expeditionary force was sent to Scotland to support the Jacobite cause. Eilean Donan was chosen as their headquarters, and was defended by a force of forty-eight Spaniards. On 10 May the castle came under attack by three English frigates – *Flamborough*, *Worcester* and *Enterprise* – commanded by Captain Boyle. The ships sailed into Loch Alsh and so up to Loch Duich, and then bombarded the castle. There was no hope of withstanding the attack, and the

Spanish garrison quickly surrendered, being taken as prisoners to Leith. The castle was left in ruins.

It remained in this sad state for 200 years. But in 1913, Lieutenant-Colonel John MacRae-Gilstrap bought the ruins and on 14 August hoisted his flag in front of a large gathering of MacRaes and local people. At the end of the First World War he returned to the castle, determined to restore it to its former magnificence. He was aided in this task by the enthusiasm and craftsmanship of Farquhar MacRae, whom he put in charge of the massive rebuilding operations. Using only the old methods of dressing stones by hand, hammering iron and working wood using the adze, and bringing all materials over from the mainland by boat (there was no bridge at this time), the castle was gradually restored. The rebuilding was done in accordance with Farquhar MacRae's instructions. He is said to have had dreams showing the castle as it once was, and he rebuilt it according to what he 'saw' in those dreams. After the work was finished, old plans of the castle were discovered among documents at Edinburgh Castle, and the castle as rebuilt was found to be identical with these. Farquhar MacRae's dreams had been accurate in every particular.

Today it is hard to imagine the castle ever having been in ruins. The barrel-vaulted ceilings, with their hundreds of hand-set stones, arch overhead and seem to emphasise the thickness of the walls. Many indications of the castle's defensive nature can still be seen today. The defences begin with the castle's island site – the stone bridge is a twentieth-century innovation; at high tide, the deep waters of the lochs surrounding the island, with their treacherous currents, would have been a substantial obstacle to overcome. Once on the island, attackers would have had sheer stone walls and a portcullis to contend with, while being showered all the while with stones, and probably, hot liquids, thrown down by the defenders on the walls above. On the lower battlements guard posts can be seen; lookouts stationed here could give early warning of an enemy's approach.

Once through the outer defences, the inner walls still provided a formidable obstacle. The walls, many feet thick; only the narrowest of window openings; the hand-wrought, heavy iron yett, which defended the main entrance and can be seen now in the Banqueting

Hall (it was found in the well during restoration); all these features show clearly how carefully thought out the defences were. The well itself was an important element, as it meant that the castle, provided with constant supplies of fresh water, could withstand a long siege. Despite the handsome, more recent, furnishings, it is easy to take an imaginary step back in time to the siege of 1539, with all its ferocity and terror.

BLAIR CASTLE

Blair Castle stands in the Strath of Garry, between the Passes of Killiecrankie and Drumochter, commanding the central route into the Highlands; it has always, therefore, had much strategic importance. The first mention of a tower on this site is in 1269, when David, Earl of Atholl, who lived much of his time in England, complained to Alexander III that John Comyn of Badenoch had moved into Atholl territory and built himself a tower at Blair.

The Earl was killed on Crusade a year later and the Comyns remained in occupation of the tower for 100 years. This tower, now called 'Cuming's Tower', is the oldest part of the present structure. In the fifteenth century, the high tower to the south-east of Cuming's Tower was built, followed in about 1530 by the dining-room, built by the third Earl. The major part of the structure was probably completed by the end of that century.

The castle was remodelled by the second Duke after the Jacobite Rising of 1745. He also removed the top storey of the castle, including the castellations and turrets. In 1869 the seventh Duke restored the tower to its original height and re-castellated the castle; he also built a new entrance, ballroom and two floors of bedrooms.

Opening times:
April–October
Daily 10.00–17.00
Tel: (01796) 481207; Fax: (01738) 481487

The Private Army

One of Blair Atholl's chief claims to fame is that it is the home of the last private army in Europe, the Atholl Highlanders. This army is the sole survivor of the old custom whereby the King of Scotland had no army, but relied on local chiefs who recognised his suzerainty to bring their clan forces to his aid.

In the Middle Ages, the army was called out on numerous occasions to support the Scottish monarch. In 1306, when the Athollmen fought for King Robert the Bruce, Earl Eoin was captured and hanged 'on a gallows thirty feet higher than usual, because of his royal descent'. In 1333, against the English again, the Earl, John Campbell, was killed.

The Lord of the Isles, MacDonald, was captured by the then Earl himself in 1475. In the counter-attack the Earl and Countess were forcibly dragged from sanctuary and only saved by a sudden storm which wrecked many Clan MacDonald galleys. For their violation of sanctuary the MacDonalds had to perform public penance in St Bride's Chapel at Blair.

A later feud developed between Atholl and Argyll, but although serious at times, the clans managed to retain a certain sense of humour in their confrontations.

It was in the seventeenth century that the strength of the Atholl forces became an important factor on a level affecting national events. On the outbreak of the Civil War the men of Atholl were called out on behalf of Charles I. It was at Blair that the King's standard was raised and for the greater part of Montrose's campaigns the castle remained a Royalist base, giving treatment to the wounded and imprisoning captives. The Athollmen, with the Irish, were the backbone of Montrose's army.

Later, the castle was occupied by Cromwellian troops, but after Atholl, with two regiments, had given his submission to General Monck, special articles allowed him and his vassals to remain in possession of their estates.

Blair once again assumed strategic importance after William of Orange had been called to the thrones of England and Scotland. Atholl and Tullibardine, his eldest son, supported William, although they had not voted to declare the throne vacant. Atholl promised the support of the Athollmen for William, if necessary, but the garrison at the castle was surprised by Stewart of Ballechin, Atholl's Bailie and a staunch Jacobite, and the castle was seized.

Murray laid siege to the castle but in the absence of artillery, he made no impression on the thick walls. After a week the siege was ordered to be raised. The Athollmen under Murray were then ordered to join the Government forces, but local loyalty to the Stuarts proved too strong; when told to give three cheers for King William, the men rushed to the near-by Banvie Burn and drank to King James, using their bonnets as cups. Murray was able only to set a guard of 100 men at the north end of the Pass of Killiecrankie to secure it for the Government troops marching north into Atholl. Even these men he thought were not to be trusted and he requested troops to reinforce them. Mackay, commander of the Government forces, was determined to secure Blair before marching further north, despite Murray's advice to avoid such strongly Jacobite territory. In the Battle of Killiecrankie which followed, although Mackay's troops got safely through the pass, Dundee's Jacobite Highland forces then swept down on them from the heights of Craig Eillaich. The Jacobites were victorious, but Dundee received wounds from which he died, to be replaced by an incompetent commander. Dundee lies buried in the Atholl family vault at St Bride's Church.

During the Jacobite Rising of 1715, the Atholl family were split in their loyalties; the Duke was a staunch Whig, but his younger brother and three of his sons joined the Jacobite army and raised four regiments in the Atholl district. With the failure of the Rising, his sons William and George fled into exile. William was later attainted and forfeited his inheritance. James, who had remained with the Duke, inherited the title and estates at his father's death.

In 1745, James, the second Duke, had to evacuate Blair at the approach of Prince Charles Edward, who had with him James's elder brother William, known as 'Duke William' by the Jacobites. William entertained the Prince at the castle, which became a centre for the Jacobite administration of their forces. William's brother George also joined the Prince's army, which was swelled by a large number of

Athollmen. The men of Atholl were now, however, being also strongly influenced by Duke James to join the Government forces. With the retreat of the Jacobite forces as support for them weakened, Blair was evacuated by Duke William and was rapidly taken over by the Government forces.

But then followed a second siege of the castle, when the Prince, hearing that Government troops were to be rallied in Atholl for a march north, ordered Lord George to attempt to recapture Blair before this concentration could take place. Duke William gave his reluctant consent to the use of red-hot cannon-balls in an attempt to set fire to the roof. He feared the destruction and irreparable loss of 'the ancestral portraits' but decided that their sacrifice for the sake of the 'Publick Service' was necessary. A board marked by one of these searingly hot cannon-balls can still be seen in the castle. The plan failed, as the Government troops armed with iron ladles scooped the cannon-balls into water-filled slop-tubs, and thus rendered them harmless. The siege was raised after two weeks. This proved to be the last formal siege of any building in Great Britain.

Sir Andrew Agnew, the Government commander who refused to surrender Blair to Lord George, was a man with great strength of character, and a violent temper. The following vivid description of the terror he struck into his subordinates was written by the eighth Duchess:

Sir Andrew Agnew indeed was as noted for his irascibility as for his dogged courage. When Lord George first arrived before the castle, he summoned the General to surrender it, but Sir Andrew's temper was so notorious that no Highlander would deliver the message. A good-looking maidservant from the Inn at Blair, who was on friendly terms with the officers, was therefore prevailed upon to take it. Waving the paper over her head as a token of her errand, she reached a low passage window at which some officers had assembled, and delivered her summons, but only a lieutenant 'with a constitution impaired by drinking' could be induced to carry it to Sir Andrew. No sooner did he begin to read it than the General drove him with fury from his presence, hurling after him such epithets against Lord George, and such threats to any other messenger he might send, that the girl herself overheard him and returned in panic to Old Blair. The officer who recorded the incident narrates that Lord George with Lord Nairn and Macpherson of Cluny could be seen waiting in the churchyard to receive her and appeared to be much amused by her report.

Sir Andrew's irascibility, however, did not deter his officers from showing him some disrespect. Borrowing one of his old uniform coats they stuffed it with straw and placed the figure at a window with a spy-glass in the hand as if reconnoitring the besiegers. The Highlanders, taken in, concentrated their fire on the window until the General's curiosity was excited and the effigy was discovered. The scandalized commandant duly instituted inquiries and the culprit confessed his guilt. Judgment was then pronounced that the 'loon' that set up the effigy must just go up himself and take it down again – not a pleasant task.

With the eventual failure of the Rising, at Culloden, Duke William was taken prisoner and died in the Tower of London. Lord George died in exile, but his son, Duke James's heir, succeeded to the title, thus making the present family descendants of both Whig and Jacobite branches.

In the eighteenth century the Athollmen gradually changed their role, as it became more common for those who wished to fight to join the regular army. They became more of a ceremonial bodyguard for the Duke, having a similar standing towards him as the Royal Company of Archers had towards the Sovereign. The greatest event in all their long history was surely the occasion, in September 1845, when Queen Victoria presented Colours to the Atholl Highlanders.

The Athollmen have provided Guards of Honour on many occasions, particularly when royal visitors have been staying at Blair Castle. They remain today unique and proud survivors of the once-numerous individual clan armies.

Dean castle

Kilmarnock is now a modern industrial town, but it still retains some vivid reminders of its colourful and turbulent past. Chief among these is Dean Castle, which has survived in a secluded valley surrounded by woodlands and greenery despite the growth of the town which now stretches out on either side of it. From the castle itself nothing of the town can be seen and the surrounding landscape, especially the thickly wooded glen of the near-by river, must look much as it did hundreds of years ago.

The keep of the castle was built in the mid fourteenth century, of sandstone with, originally, a thatched roof, which has since been replaced by slates. The main part of the castle, known as the 'Place' (or Palace) was built about 1460, and the buildings visible today are much as they would have been in medieval times.

Dean Castle is now in the care of Kilmarnock and Loudoun District Council.

The story which follows was written by Mr James Hunter, Curator of Dean Castle.

Opening times:
All year, daily 10.00–17.00

The Legend of the Lord Kilmarnock's Head

For 450 years Dean Castle was the stronghold of the Boyd family, whose adventurous and violent history saw them taking part in wars, intrigues and feuds throughout the centuries. Many episodes from the days of the Boyds make stories full of excitement and romance but none is more dramatic than that of William, fourth Earl of Kilmarnock, last of the Boyds to make Dean Castle his home.

The disasters which befell the unfortunate Earl began in 1735 with a fire which ravaged much of Dean Castle and left the main residential building, the Place, a roofless ruin. The Earl was already in financial difficulty and unable to have the damage repaired. However, although he also had another property, Kilmarnock House, at the other end of the town, he continued to make use of the remaining buildings at Dean Castle. So it was here that there occurred the strange and horrifying event which was to prove prophetic of the fate of the Earl himself. The story was first revealed by the Earl to his friend, the Earl of Galloway, and was thus recorded not long after:

About a year before the Rebellion, as the Earl of Kilmarnock was one day walking in his garden, he was suddenly alarmed with a fearful shriek, which, while he was reflecting on it with astonishment, was soon after repeated. On this, he went into the house, and enquired of his lady and all the servants, without being able to discover from whom or whence the cry proceeded. But missing his lady's woman, he was informed that she had gone into an upper room to inspect some linen, whereupon the Earl and his lady went up and opened the door, which was only latched, but no sooner did the gentlewoman within set her eyes on his lordship's face than she fainted away. When, with proper assistance, she was brought to herself, they asked her the meaning of what they had heard and seen. She replied that while she sat sewing some linen she had taken up to mend, the door opened of itself and a bloody head entered the room and rolled on the floor; that this dreadful sight made her cry out, but it instantly disappeared; that in a few moments she saw the same

33

apparition again, on which she repeated her shrieks; and at the third time she fainted away, and was but just recovered when she saw his lordship coming in, which had made the impression on her they had been witness to. This relation given by the affrighted gentlewoman was only laughed at and ridiculed as the effect of spleen, vapours, or the strength of a deluded imagination, and was thought no more of till one night when my Lord Kilmarnock happened to tell the story to the Earl of Galloway, the subject of their lordships' conversation happening to be on spectres and apparitions, the vulgar notions of which they were ridiculing. But after Kilmarnock had engaged in the Rebellion and Lord Galloway was told of it, he instantly recollected this story and said, 'I'll lay a wager that Kilmarnock will lose his head.'

The circumstances in which this came about are tinged with tragic irony. The Earl of Kilmarnock's first acquaintance with war had been in 1715 when, at the age of ten, he rode with his father at the head of a detachment of 340 men, raised in Kilmarnock to support the Government against the Jacobite Rising. Why, with this family background, the fourth Earl should have himself joined the next Jacobite Rising led by Bonnie Prince Charlie in 1745, has never been properly explained. Perhaps it was because he hoped for financial gain to restore his family fortunes, or perhaps it was the influence of his wife, Lady Anne Livingstone, who came from a Jacobite family. The Boyd family was divided, for the Earl's eldest son, James, fought on the Government side, while his second son, Charles, followed his father, fighting with him at the Battle of Culloden on 16 April 1746.

After the defeat of the Jacobite army, Charles escaped abroad, but the Earl was captured when he mistook a troop of Government cavalry for Jacobites. Being recognised by an officer, he was in fact captured alive instead of being butchered like the ordinary Jacobite prisoners.

The story is told of how he was led, dishevelled and bareheaded, before the ranks of the Royal Scots Fusiliers, in which his son James served. As he passed, his son stepped forward and, without saying a word, placed his own hat on his father's head.

The Earl was held prisoner in the Tower of London and tried along with two other captured Jacobite commanders, the Earl of Cromarty and Lord Balmerino. The trial took place before the House of Lords at the end of July and was a travesty of justice. The charge was High Treason, and it was claimed that the accused deserved death because they had ordered the Jacobite army to give no quarter to Government troops.

This was quite untrue; no such order had been given by anyone and indeed Lord Kilmarnock had personally intervened with Prince Charles before the Battle of Culloden to secure better treatment for the prisoners then held. Considering the barbarous behaviour of the Government troops towards Jacobite prisoners after Culloden, it was a final irony that the Earl of Kilmarnock was sentenced to death for what would now be termed war crimes he certainly did not commit.

Despite a most eloquent speech by Lord Kilmarnock, sentence was pronounced on all three prisoners, but Lord Cromarty was pardoned.

On Monday, 18 August 1746, Lords Kilmarnock and Balmerino were beheaded on Tower Hill in London before a great crowd of spectators. All were struck by the courageous bearing of the two noblemen, Lord Balmerino seeming completely indifferent to death and Lord Kilmarnock quietly composed. But before the execution took place, Lord Kilmarnock insisted on special arrangements being made. Four men were detailed to stand with a large cloth, ready to catch the Earl's head, because the Earl said that while he could face death with calmness, he could not face the thought of his head rolling about on the scaffold covered in blood. Was he then thinking of the frightening apparition that had appeared in his home?

hopetoun house

Hopetoun House, near South Queensferry in West Lothian, stands in 100 acres of beautiful parkland overlooking the Forth Estuary. The two famous Forth bridges can be seen to the east.

Hopetoun is the ancestral home of the Marquess of Linlithgow, and it is one of the finest houses of its period in Scotland. The building of the house was begun in 1699, for the first Earl of Hopetoun, by Sir William Bruce (who was the architect responsible for Holyrood Palace). However, from 1721 until 1767, it was enlarged by William Adam and his sons, John and the better-known Robert. John and Robert were also concerned with the interior decoration of the most important apartments, and much of the original furniture still survives today. Also in these splendid apartments hang paintings by many notable artists, including the School of Rubens, Canaletto, Passerotti and Teniers. Among the many other treasures to be found in the house is a museum of social history which has among its exhibits costumes, china and documents.

Hopetoun House Preservation Trust

Opening times:
Early April – early October; other dates by appointment
Daily 10.00–17.30
Tel: (0131) 331 2451; Fax: (0131) 319 1885

Hopetoun House is, on the whole, a very happy home, but there is one tale which is imbued with terror. It is related here by the Marquess of Linlithgow.

There is a particular path, in the grounds of Hopetoun, which as children, for some reason or another, my sisters and brother and I always used to avoid. We had no particular reason for doing so except that we were always frightened of it. It was many years after we grew up that we were told the story which may or may not have had something to do with our fears, although, of course, we knew nothing about it when we were young.

The tradition is that on a number of occasions a dark, robed figure has been seen in the area. This ghostly apparition always coincides with some misfortune, usually a death in the family, almost immediately after the visitation.

The only incident which I can vouch for is that one day we were walking in the area with our dogs when, to our horror, they began growling and barking, and were obviously following something that they could see and we could not. One of them was even trying to snap at a pair of invisible ankles. Certainly, disaster followed within forty-eight hours, and ever since that day I have avoided the area as much as possible. If I do have to take that particular path, I move with considerable speed and am very glad when I am past a particular tree, after which all sensations of fear disappear.

Dunvegan Castle

Dunvegan Castle, home of the Chiefs of Clan MacLeod for over 750 years, stands on a bare volcanic rock at the heart of Loch Dunvegan. During the thirteenth century, in the time of Leod, the eponymous chief of the clan, a curtain-wall was built and parts of this still survive. A massive keep was added in the fourteenth century and in the next century was built the four-storey Fairy Tower which survives virtually intact.

As the need for strong defences receded, so the uncomfortable keep was abandoned, in the seventeenth century, and the building of a new hall began. An extended south wing was later added. In the eighteenth century came new kitchens, outhouses and a barrack block, and the keep was restored. However, between 1810 and 1846 the castle was 'modernised', entailing the destruction of much of the earlier work.

After a fire in 1939 Dame Flora, twenty-eighth Chief, had the south wing remodelled and, also in her time, the castle was opened to the public. On her death in 1976, her grandson, John, succeeded her as twenty-ninth Chief. He has rearranged and redecorated the rooms viewed by the public and has added an exhibition room and shop on the ground floor. His own family's living-quarters are on the second floor.

The stories which follow were written by Ruairidh H. MacLeod, F.S.A. (Scot.), Editor of Clan MacLeod Magazine.

Opening times:
Late March–October; other dates by appointment
Mon–Sat 10.00–17.30,
Sun 13.00–17.30 (gardens, craft shops and restaurants from 10.00)
Tel: (01470) 521206; Fax: (01470) 521205

The Curse of the MacLeods

From at least the end of the seventeenth century there was a prophecy concerning the MacLeods at Dunvegan that 'when Norman, the fourth Norman, the son of a hard, slender English lady would perish by an accidental death; that when the "Maidens" of MacLeod became the property of a Campbell; when a fox had young ones in one of the turrets of the Castle, and particularly when the fairy-enchanted banner should be for the last time exhibited, then the glory of the MacLeod's family should depart – a great part of the estate should be sold to others; so that a small boat would carry all the gentlemen of the name MacLeod across Loch Dunvegan; but that in times far distant a chief named "Speckled" John (Iain Breac) should arise, who should redeem those estates, and raise the powers and honour of the house to higher pitch than ever before.'

In 1799 Norman MacLeod, twenty-third Chief, had already earned himself fame and fortune as a General in India. His visits to Dunvegan were rare, since he was also a Member of Parliament, but in that year he returned to his ancestral home. On the way north he stopped at Morvern to call on his old tutor, the Reverend Norman MacLeod, and insisted on taking the latter's sixteen-year-old son, Norman, on to Dunvegan with him. The boy spent three happy months in the castle, sleeping in a small room next to the Chief's. The lad was to become famous as the minister of St Columba's Church, Glasgow, and Moderator of the General Assembly, and loved as *Caraid nan Gaidheal*, the Friend of the Gael. He was born in the manse at Fuinary and is the ancestor of the Very Reverend Lord MacLeod of Fuinary.

Caraid nan Gaidheal later wrote that 'There was at that time, at Dunvegan, an English smith, with whom I became a favourite, and who told me, in solemn secrecy, that the iron chest which contained the "Fairy Flag" was to be forced open the next morning.' Norman was sworn to secrecy by the Chief's Edinburgh lawyer, Mr Buchanan, who was at Dunvegan, and ordered to keep the event a 'profound secret' from the Chief.

With great violence the smith duly tore open the chest, and inside 'was found the flag, enclosed in a wooden box of strongly scented wood'. The Fairy Flag consisted of 'a square piece of very rich silk, with crosses wrought in gold thread, and several elf-spots stitched with great care on different parts of it'.

Within a week news reached Dunvegan of the death of the Chief's eldest son Norman, blown up in the vessel H.M.S. *Charlotte*, when it exploded. Had this Norman lived, he would have been the fourth successive Chief to bear the name.

Soon after, to meet General MacLeod's ever-increasing debts, the house and farm of Orbost, four miles south of Dunvegan, were sold to Angus Campbell of Ensay. Included in the sale were the sea stacks off Idrigill Point called 'MacLeod's Maidens'. At about the same time a Lieutenant MacLean, who was billeted in the barrack block of the castle, produced a tame vixen which had pups in one of the castle's towers.

'And thus', concluded *Caraid nan Gaidheal*, 'all that was in the prophecy alluded to was literally fulfilled.'

The Isle of Harris had been sold in 1779; Skeabost, Trumpan and Lynedale in 1781; Stein and Lusta in 1790; Waternish, Greshornish, Isay and Mingay in 1797. In 1799 as well as Orbost, Colbost, Skinidin, part of Glendale and Husabost were sold, and finally in 1811 Glenelg on the mainland was to be sold.

Within fifty years large boats had carried thousands of MacLeod tacksmen and tenants to Canada, America, Australia and New Zealand, and no more than a handful bearing the name MacLeod were left at Dunvegan.

The General died very suddenly at the age of forty-seven in 1801; his surviving son died at the same age in 1835; the General's grandson, in an attempt to alleviate the destitution on his estates during the potato famine of the late 1840s, brought the family near to ruin by selling all the movables, letting the castle, and taking a job in London.

This Chief, also called Norman, had four sons, one of whom died young, but none were survived by male heirs. Two sons, Norman Magnus and Sir Reginald, succeeded as Chief, and the third, Roderick, had a son, the heir apparent, who was killed at Givenchy serving with the Black Watch in 1915. In 1920 Norman Magnus, twenty-sixth Chief, with the agreement of his brothers, sold to the Government the parish of Bracadale and Minginish, retaining only the land round the castle and the Black Cullins.

In 1935 the direct male line of the MacLeods, who had been in possession of Dunvegan Castle for 700 years, died out. There was not a single gentleman of the name MacLeod left to row a boat across Loch Dunvegan.

Sir Reginald was succeeded by his elder daughter, Flora, whom the clan then accepted as their Chief. This lady was to put new meaning into the title 'Clan Chief'. Dame Flora MacLeod of MacLeod, at the age of fifty-seven, having already lived a full life, began reviving the interest and loyalty of her scattered clan family. Her name became a household word, so that all over the English-speaking world there were people who believed that they had a granny called MacLeod. The idea of reuniting and visiting her dispersed clan had been inspired by the visits made to Dunvegan Castle during the Second World War by overseas servicemen. Dame Flora founded Clan MacLeod Societies in Canada, America, Australia and New Zealand where she travelled extensively. Chief for more than forty years, she died in 1976 at the age of ninety-eight.

The Fairy Flag
Despite the breaking of the iron box and the 'waving' of the Fairy Flag in 1799, Dame Flora wrote: 'I firmly believe that the magic is still there and that the Flag does guard the Castle and the Clan. This thought gave great comfort to our young clansmen serving in the war. They took away pictures in their pocket-books and considered them as talismen.' She added that 'The Fairy Flag is very, very exciting because, as you know, it must always be a mystery.'

Norman MacLeod, *Caraid nan Gaidheal*, wrote of the Fairy Flag that 'After being carefully examined, it was restored to its case as before, bits were taken away from time to time, and I imagine that now none of it is left.' The earliest Clan MacLeod history, written about 1829, states that 'the flag which was once large is reduced', and the historian added 'I possess a fragment.' Certainly none of the 'crosses wrought in gold' have survived.

45

It was not until 1922 that the Fairy Flag was mounted under glass and put on display in the castle. What remains of the Flag is a tattered rectangle of oatmeal-coloured silk, about forty-five inches high and twenty inches broad. On the right a hem has been formed wide enough to contain the banner staff. There are a number of small darns, and two large 'elf-spots' carefully worked in red silk.

There are at least seven traditions of how the Fairy Flag came to Dunvegan Castle.

The Fairy Flag and the Holy Land

Three of the traditions concern a MacLeod, or a MacLeod Chief, in the Holy Land. In the first, a priest acquired the Fairy Flag, by killing a witch who wore the cloth as a garment to make her invisible. In the second a MacLeod Chief armed with a piece of the True Cross defeated a she-devil, the Daughter of Thunder, in a mountain pass. In dying, she revealed to him the future destinies of the Clan and directed him to make a banner from her girdle and a staff from her spear. In the third, the MacLeod hero fought a fairy in mid-stream while crossing a river, and having finally overpowered the fairy, she became friendly, and gave him a present of a set of fitting boxes containing a magic flag. 'If you or your people are ever in sore peril, wave the flag and many armed men will immediately come to your need. But do not open the box for the present, not for a year and a day; for if you do no corn will grow, no sheep or cattle have young, no children will be born, in your country for another year.' He returned to Skye with the box, curiosity overcame his wife, and she opened the box with dire results. The Chief then took the flag and had a strong iron box made for it and appointed a family to take care of it.

The late Seton Gordon gave a tradition that MacDiarmid, a ploughman, was given a present of a Fairy Flag for the Chief by a fairy. Lady MacLeod had to see the Flag. 'Now the flag had a gift and that was to let you see all the people in the world when you look at it.' Lady Macleod, who was pregnant, 'got such a fright on seeing the Flag, that she gave birth right away, and every cow, mare, sheep and pig in the area had their young before their time at that very moment.'

The Fairy Flag and the Fairy Lullaby

There are three traditions connecting the Fairy Flag with the Fairy Lullaby and the young MacLeod heir. The Fairy Lullaby, a poem in archaic Gaelic, praises the race of Leod descended from the Kings of Norway. It was often sung by the late Alice, Mrs Macnab of Macnab, Dame Flora's elder daughter.

In the first tradition a beautiful fairy, dressed in green, entered the nursery of the castle through closed doors and took the baby on her knee, while the nurse remained immobile, and sang the lullaby. On hearing the song Lady MacLeod went into the room, traditionally the Fairy Room on the second floor of the Fairy Tower, and called out, 'God save us, it is I who am the mother of yon child.' At the sound of the Good Name, the fairy disappeared leaving the Fairy Flag, and the memory of the lullaby.

In the second tradition, the nurse, growing impatient at being shut up with the baby during the christening festivities, left her charge and joined the rest of the clan in the Hall. After kicking off his blanket the child grew cold and, crying out, a fairy, who was keeping watch over him, covered the boy with a fairy cloth. Meanwhile down below, the clansfolk clamoured to see the heir, and when the nurse was found, she was sent to fetch him and returned to the Hall with the child wrapped in the magic cloth, and accompanied by a chorus of fairy voices which sang of the virtues of the Flag, and the good it would bring the clan in battle.

A third tradition tells of the child and nurse being kidnapped by the fairies and taken into one of their underground forts. By chance a shepherdess one day came with her flock to a spot just above the fort. Seated on the ground while mending her dress, she heard fairies singing the lullaby, and placing her ear to the ground heard the words. She told the Chief where the child was hidden, but nothing was done to rescue the baby, who would be well guarded by the fairies, until Hallowe'en, when it was well known that all fairies left their forts to go dancing. On the appropriate evening the clan went to the fort and rescued the child, who was wrapped in the Fairy Flag, and the nurse, who sang the Fairy Lullaby.

The Chief's Fairy Wife

The last tradition tells that Malcolm, third Chief, who died about 1370 went off to Fairy Land where he married a fairy and lived with her for twenty years. There is also a tradition that she lived with him at Dunvegan for twenty years. The two parted at what is now called Fairy Bridge, three miles east of the Castle. On bidding her earthly husband farewell, she gave him the Fairy Flag, instructing him to keep it carefully, and that when he was hard pressed in battle, the waving of the Flag would bring a host of armed men to his aid.

Whatever the traditional origins of the Fairy Flag 'the honour and very existence of the Clan MacLeod was supposed for ages to depend almost entirely on its preservation. The highest and purest blood of the race, as well as the most renowned and powerful heroes, were selected to guard it, if necessity called for display.'

One family of MacLeods were Hereditary Keepers of the Flag for three centuries and had a special tomb at Rodel in Harris. Members of the family bore the Flag in battle, surrounded by twelve stout men each holding in one hand a golden cord attached to the staff, and in their other hand a drawn sword. The Flag was placed immediately behind the Chief.

According to the earliest history of the MacLeods, written about 1829, 'the charm attached to this banner was to vanish on its third display, when one of two things was to happen; viz. a complete victory of the clan over their foes; or their total extinction for ever. This trial was always avoided nor is there much likelihood, now, of its ever being attempted.'

The Fairy Flag has been waved in battle twice, on both occasions against the MacDonalds of Clanranald, at the Battle of Glendale in about 1490 and at the Battle of Trumpan in about 1530, when the MacLeods were victorious. There is also a tradition that the Fairy Flag was waved at the Battle of Bloody Day in about 1480, after the MacLeod Chief had been killed. But since William 'Longsword' was still alive fifteen years later, and this was not strictly a MacLeod Clan battle, it is generally discounted. It was not waved at the Battle of the Cuillins in 1601 (when the MacDonalds of Sleat defeated the MacLeods) perhaps because of the fear of the result of the third wave.

There is also a tradition that the Flag was waved to cure a murrain among the cattle, which it did.

The Chiefs of the Clan continued firmly to believe in the magic of the Flag. In 1922 the Fairy Flag was sent to London to be examined at the Victoria and Albert Museum. In the opinion of the expert, Mr Wace, the silk had been made in Rhodes or Syria, in the tenth or eleventh centuries, and the red darns, hitherto called 'elf-spots', were of the same age as the silk, suggesting that the Flag had been a prized possession, lovingly mended, and perhaps a holy relic, like the shirt of a saint. On hearing this opinion Sir Reginald, Dame Flora's father, replied: 'Mr Wace, you think that, but I *know* that it was given to my ancestor by a fairy', to which Mr Wace replied, 'Sir Reginald, I bow to your superior knowledge.'

The Fairy Flag and Landravager
The traditions of the Flag might be the end of the tale, were it not that it *is* made of silk which is a thousand years old, and that the magic banner had the same properties as a very famous Viking flag.

Harald Hardrada had fought, as a young boy, at the Battle of Stilestad in 1030, when his half-brother, St Olaf, was killed. He fled to Russia where he served King Yaroslav of Kiev. Harald then joined the Varangian Guard of the Byzantine Emperor Michael IV at Constantinople – 'Fairy Land' to anyone who had not been there – and fought in Sicily and Bulgaria. He is even said to have made a pilgrimage to Jerusalem. After an affair with the Emperor's wife, he returned to Kiev, where he married Elisabeth, daughter of King Yaroslav. In 1045 he returned to Norway, where his nephew Magnus was King. Magnus was so impressed with the treasure that Harald had collected, that he agreed to give Harald half his kingdom, if he received half Harald's treasure.

One of Harald's friends asked him which treasure he valued most highly, and he answered that above all else he valued his banner, Landravager, for whoever marched under Landravager marched to victory.

In 1047 Harald became sole ruler of Norway when his nephew was killed fighting King Svein of Denmark. Harald spent the next fifteen years attempting to add Denmark to his possessions, but failed. However, he successfully annexed Shetland, Orkney and the Hebrides to Norway.

In 1066 Harald launched an expedition to conquer England. With only a small force, while his army was resting, and with Landravager still with the Viking ships, Harald was surprised at Stamford Bridge, in Yorkshire, by Harold Godwinson's celebrated forced march from London, and was killed. The Norwegians were scattered and Landravager disappeared.

Godred Crovan was one of the men closely associated with Harald Hardrada, and may possibly have been his son. He was at the Battle of Stamford Bridge and fled via the Northern Isles to Man, where he eventually seized the throne. It is believed that he took Landravager with him. He founded a royal house, from which the MacLeods, through their eponymous Chief Leod, claim descent.

Could the Fairy Flag, made in Rhodes or Syria in the tenth or eleventh centuries, and lovingly mended and kept as a holy relic, have passed to the MacLeods from the Isle of Man and been Harald Hardrada's Landravager, acquired in Constantinople or Kiev more than 900 years ago? Dame Flora concluded that 'the experts say you cannot possibly prove it, but it is a perfectly possible explanation'.

One puzzle concerning this explanation is that the Fairy Flag was mentioned in battles which occurred in about 1480, 1490 and 1530, and the standard-bearers were first mentioned in 1480. If the Chiefs had had the Flag for 200 years before that, why was it never mentioned before? And why was it used twice or even three times out of a possible three so soon after being first mentioned? There is a tradition that the Fairy Flag was brought back from a Crusade, but it seems unlikely that a MacLeod Chief or one of his clansmen could have done so, since the last Christian strongholds of Tripoli and Acre fell in 1289–91. The Fairy Flag might have been a holy relic salvaged from the Fall of Constantinople in 1453 and brought west to find its way to Skye by the end of the fifteenth century.

Dame Flora certainly believed in the magic of the Fairy Flag and always bid her clansfolk greet it when visiting the castle. In August 1956 when Her Majesty Queen Elizabeth II was to visit Dunvegan, the west coast was lashed by storms, so that the Queen was forced to abandon a call at Mull. People in Skye were fearful that the Queen would not be able to land at Dunvegan, but Dame Flora was quietly confident. 'It will be fine for the Queen's visit. I have spoken to the Fairy Flag.' And fine it was, a windy but bright sunny day. After lunching in the castle the Queen met clansfolk who had gathered from all over the world to celebrate Dame Flora's grandson's coming of age, in the Guncourt of the castle.

The Silver Chanter of the MacCrimmons

The Guncourt was the scene of another traditional story of Dunvegan Castle, set in the early seventeenth century.

Wherever pipers have played together, there have been competitions. *Alasdair Crotach*, eighth Chief, established a college of piping at Boreraig on the other side of Loch Dunvegan, and then invited a dozen neighbouring Highland chiefs to bring their pipers to Dunvegan for a competition. The Chief must have been confident that his MacCrimmon piper would be victorious. As the host's piper he was to play last.

The Great Hall in the keep at Dunvegan was packed with boastful chiefs and their eminent clansmen. Piper after piper swept into the smoky room, fingering his chanter with the utmost skill and playing piercing laments or rousing salutes. Down below in the kitchens, those who had played relaxed as the whisky was passed round. Those who still had to play were busy tuning their pipes.

Later in the evening MacLeod's worried Chamberlain crept into the hall to inform his Chief that the clan's piper would be incapable of playing, for he had drunk, or been made to drink, too much whisky. After quick consultation Alasdair Crotach decided that the honour of the clan must be maintained, and that a piper must play. MacCrimmon's young son would have to play in his father's stead.

The young boy, a promising though uninspired player, had been hanging round the kitchens listening to the pipers tuning up. Suddenly he found himself ordered to play for his Chief. He, a mere learner, had to represent his clan, the greatest in the land, before the chiefs of a dozen others.

The young boy ran out into the Guncourt, threw himself upon the ground, and wept. After a few moments, he felt a tap on the shoulder, and looking up he saw a little lady dressed in green, and since fairies in Skye were well known to wear green, the boy knew at once who she must be.

The fairy asked the Boy, 'Which would you rather; pipe badly but be acclaimed great, or be a great piper and unrecognised.' The boy considered the question and replied that he wished to be a great piper, but that this was not possible, since the music was not in him. Then the fairy offered the boy a magic silver chanter on condition that the boy came when called and that he would always treat and speak to the chanter with the respect due to a lady. The boy accepted the conditions and received the silver chanter.

Young MacCrimmon marched proudly into the Hall of the castle to play for his Chief, but was greeted with howls of derision by the assembled company. This soon changed, however, to cries of amazement and wonder as magical music poured out of the boy's pipes. MacLeod's piper was unanimously acclaimed the winner by all the chiefs.

The family of the MacCrimmons were hereditary pipers to the Chiefs of the MacLeods for almost three centuries, and were recognised as the 'Princes of Pipers' throughout the kingdom. Their college was attended by pupils from Argyll, Inverness and Sutherland.

In his time MacCrimmon was called by the fairy and disappeared into a cave at Harlosh. The silver chanter continued in his family for many generations until one day, when crossing by boat from Raasay in cold, wet weather, the Chief having ordered MacCrimmon to play a rousing tune, the piper, with numb fingers, inadvertently swore at the chanter which slipped off his pipes and fell into the sea.

In 1967 Dame Flora, with the help of Seumas MacNeill and John MacFadyen, instituted the MacCrimmon Memorial Piobaireachd Competition for a prize of a Silver Chanter, in order to attract back to Dunvegan, the cradle of classic bagpipe music, the best piobaireachd players in the world.

BRODie castle

Brodie Castle is situated between Nairn and Forres, just to the north of the Muckle Water which flows down to Findhorn Bay. The castle has been the seat of the ancient family of Brodie since the eleventh century, but the history of the early Brodies is scarce, mostly as a result of action taken by Lord Lewis Gordon, one of Montrose's brilliant young generals, during a campaign in 1645. Gordon sacked many houses in the area and set fire to Brodie, causing little structural damage but destroying nearly all the family papers and documents.

These records, of course, could not be replaced but the castle itself was fairly easily restored, with most of the surviving structure being incorporated in the rebuilding. The earliest part of the present castle is the tower, which dates from the fifteenth century. An important feature of the interior is a valuable collection of English and Dutch paintings. Brodie Castle is now the property of the National Trust for Scotland.

The stories which follow were written by Brodie of Brodie.

The National Trust for Scotland

Opening times:
April–September (early October Sat and Sun only)
Mon–Sat 11.00–17.30, Sun 14.00–17.30
Grounds open all year 09.30–sunset
Tel: (01309) 641371

Alexander Brodie and the beggar

Alexander Brodie of Brodie lived from 1617 to 1680. He was a fanatical Presbyterian, and in 1640 led the party which caused havoc in Elgin Cathedral, destroying stone- and wood-carvings, and its paintings of the Crucifixion and the Last Judgment. Ten years later, he was one of those sent by the General Assembly to persuade Charles II to sign the National Covenant, and to invite him to Scotland as King.

He is the author of a remarkable set of diaries, published in the last century, which reflect the strength of his religious beliefs. So convinced was he in the power of prayer that when he was told of a beggar's arrival at his door, he went to the man, and, looking up to Heaven, he prayed at length for the relief of the poor wretch's suffering. In fact, he prayed for so long that when he looked round him again, the beggar had gone, obviously tired of waiting, in search of quicker charity!

Fire at Brodie

Luckily, there has been little in the way of tragedy in the history of Brodie, but in 1786 such an event occurred. An account of the dreadful happenings was written soon after:

'... They returned next morning to Brodie House and found Lady Margaret in uncommon good spirits which she kept up the whole day, the evening at cards, and at supper. The gentlemen, being sleepy, proposed going to bed about eleven o'clock, when Mr Brodie attended her to her room, saw she had a good fire, and returned to see the gentlemen to their beds, from which he immediately went to his own. The instant he lay down, he fell asleep, from which he was soon awakened by the most dismal shrieks, which still vibrate in his ears. He rushed downstairs, and, in the passage from her dressing-room to the bedchamber, was met by the flames. At the risk of his life, and being burnt in the hand and leg, he pushed forward and sought the dear unfortunate in vain. Suffocation and flame drove him back to the passage to recover his breath, then, frantic, he again pushed in, for the whole room to the very cornice and furniture was in a blaze, and in his second attempt, found the lovely sufferer on the floor. . . . Oh! What a sight was here, the lovely, the once-admired Lady Margaret in a few minutes a disfigured corpse, for death and the element had done their work. . . . From the most minute investigation it appears that she immediately sent away her maid and sat down before the fire with a volume of Dodd's works, that she fell asleep, and that a peat fell on her petticoat which set her on a blaze. She must have run to the bed to which she communicated it, for it was at the foot of it she was found. Her suffering could not have been long, as her piercing cries preceded suffocation. Her child, Charlotte, who was her bedfellow, escaped downstairs, nobody knows how. My poor friend's distress beggars description. . . . The last duties are to be performed on Friday, to which sad time I look forward with horror. It is not with callous heart that I have given you this affecting detail. It seems to me that you would be anxious to know it, and that few had access to inform you with truth. . . . That Heaven may avert such judgement from you and yours and grant you all happiness is, Madam, my dearest prayer. . . .'

Lady Margaret's bedroom, a small room in the oldest part of the castle, suffered little damage, and has been used as a children's play-room this century. Her ghost has never been heard or seen, so we can only assume that her soul rests in peace after her terrible end.

The death of Hugh Brodie
Readers of the *Nairnshire Telegraph* on 25 September 1889 might have noticed the following article: 'The sad intelligence of the death of Brodie of Brodie, which reached Nairn on Sunday forenoon, profoundly affected the people of this whole district. . . . Brodie left this country about the beginning of August, and went by medical advice to take the baths at Aix-les-Bains. His health was thereby greatly benefited, and his medical advisers hoped for complete restoration. . . .' He travelled on to Switzerland 'where the neuralgic pains at the heart from which he suffered once more returned . . .'.

Meanwhile, as its master was abroad, Brodie Castle had been let, the tenants having the run of most of the rooms, with the exception of Hugh's business-room, which was in a small wing. During the evening of 20 September, the butler announced to the tenants: 'There is someone in the Master's study!' Sure enough, although the only door to the room was securely locked, sounds could be heard of papers being shuffled and someone appeared to be moaning inside. Next day, the first news of Hugh's death the previous afternoon was heard, and it is fair to assume that the residents of the castle were 'profoundly affected' by it!

The ghost made only the one visit, however, and was never heard again.

The Spiral Staircase

When the main front stairway was constructed at some time during the eighteenth century, a spiral staircase was removed from the corner turret of one of the towers, as it was slightly unsafe, and no longer needed. During the course of its removal, the skeleton of a young child was found, the origins of whom were then, and are still, unknown. The bones were placed in a glass-fronted cabinet, which now stands in the Charter Room, a small windowless area, where all the family documents are kept. Visitors are sometimes told of the 'skeleton in the cupboard', but little expect it to be literally true!

Where the spiral stair used to run is now a hollow turret, and it was here, in Edwardian days, that the English butler pointed, and said in his broad Cockney accent: 'This is where they used to 'ang 'em!' Needless to say, no one ever was hanged there, and although the Scottish Chiefs held the power of 'pit and gallows' over their clansmen, there is no record of this prerogative being enforced at Brodie.

The discovery of the Brodie Pontifical

The story of one of the most inexplicable 'finds' of modern times begins in 1970, when Mrs Helena Brodie of Brodie decided to look in the Old Stables at Brodie for a chair which she might match with three others in her home. The stables had not been explored for many years, although they were known to contain a lot of junk, and some 'rubbishy old books'. Mrs Brodie did not find the matching chair, but, beneath a pigeon's nest, she found the books. She realised at once that they were old and took them down for inspection. Five volumes of seventeenth-century atlases caused immediate interest, but the value of the Pontifical was not immediately appreciated. The Reverend George Sessford, then Episcopal Rector of St John's, Forres, and now Bishop of Moray, knew at once that it was a book of some importance, and it was finally identified and authenticated by the National Library in Edinburgh as a previously unrecorded tenth-century English religious manuscript, a working Pontifical, a book which only a Bishop would have used.

Experts called it the most important find of its kind this century. Only six comparable manuscripts of this period are known to have survived, and they are all housed in State Collections, mainly in France, Sotheby's, who sold the Pontifical the following year, said: 'It is extraordinarily rare. This sort of thing has never turned up before. . . . What is so extraordinary is that a manuscript of this importance should have been lying for so long undiscovered in a Scottish castle. Nobody has yet been able to establish how it got there.' To this day no one has come up with a logical answer as to how such valuable property lay for so long in the stables, and the mystery will probably never be solved.

The Pontifical is now in the British Museum.

glamis castle

Glamis Castle, which stands in fine grounds bordered by the Dean Water, is a graceful, romantic edifice built of warm pink stone. With its rounded turrets, castellations and conical spires, it is reminiscent of the illuminations in a French medieval Book of Hours. Indeed, the châteaux of the Loire inspired its present form, which was a result of rebuilding work in the seventeenth century. This was a period when many castles in Scotland flowered, or were enlarged and beautified in this style.

There has been a castle on this site since earliest recorded history, and the claim is made that Glamis is the oldest continually inhabited castle in the country. The central, older portion may date from as early as the eleventh century. Glamis Castle is the home of the Earls of Strathmore, and has royal associations – it was the Queen Mother's childhood home, and Princess Margaret was born here.

Opening times:
Early April – late October; other dates by appointment
Daily 10.30–17.30
Tel: (01307) 840242, 840393; Fax: (01307) 840257

Perhaps the most famous association that the name of Glamis conjures up is that of Macbeth. In Shakespeare's play, Macbeth was the Thane of Glamis. It seems likely that Macbeth was a historical figure – a King in Scotland in the eleventh century, but his identity as Thane of Glamis is questionable. However, this doubt does not reduce the power of the play, and the events which occur in it are typical of the savagery and intrigue of earlier centuries.

This tragic tale of ambition and wickedness and almost unrelieved evil is set mainly at Macbeth's castle. The triple prophecy of the three witches, that Macbeth will become Thane of Cawdor, then King of Scotland, but that the heirs of Banquo, not his heirs, will reign after him, is revealed to Macbeth and his friend Banquo on a moor near by. When Macbeth does, by chance, become Thane of Cawdor, he is persuaded by his wife to take steps to make the rest of the prophecy come true, and he assassinates King Duncan at the castle. The killing of King Duncan is followed by the murder of Banquo and the shocking massacre of Lady Macduff, the wife of a rival, and her children, as Macbeth's ambition mounts, fired by his wife and the witches' words. The story progresses with doom-ridden logic to the madness and death of Lady Macbeth. Macbeth becomes King, but abandons Glamis, with its horrifying associations, for near-by Dunsinane Castle. Fulfilling the witches prophecy he meets his death at the hands of Macduff, when Dunsinane Wood (in fact an army camouflaged with branches) rises and he is killed in battle.

Whether Macbeth was really Thane of Glamis or whether Shakespeare used artistic licence in placing the events within the walls of the castle, nevertheless the room in the central tower where Duncan is said to have been murdered certainly has a very sinister atmosphere. But even without Macbeth as an ancestor, the royal connections of the Bowes Lyon family go back far into history. In 1376 Sir John Lyon of Forteviot, made Thane of Glamis in 1372, married the Princess Joanna, daughter of King Robert II. His son, John, married his cousin, Elizabeth Graham, a granddaughter of Robert II.

The close association with the Royal Family continued through the next century, but when James V became King his hatred for the Douglas family led to the souring of relations with the Lyon family, as the then Lady Glamis was a Douglas. This unfortunate lady was accused of witchcraft and was burnt alive on the Castle Hill at Edinburgh.

Relations later improved, the eighth Lord Glamis being Chancellor for Scotland and his son a Privy Councillor, who was created Earl of Kinghorne. The second Earl was a close friend of Montrose, but later gave large sums of money to support the Covenanters against him, when he felt Montrose had taken a mistaken path. His son, the third Earl, had to retrieve the estate from vast debts as a result of this financial support for the Covenanters, but his 'prudence and frugality' achieved not only the survival but the enlargement of the castle and improvement of the estate. He obtained a new charter, by which he and his heirs were to be styled Earl of Strathmore and Kinghorne.

The family name became Bowes Lyon when the ninth Earl married the heiress Mary Eleanor Bowes, of an old North of England family, whose ancestors included one of Queen Elizabeth I's Ambassadors.

The royal connections of the family were renewed when the youngest daughter of the fourteenth Earl and Countess, Lady Elizabeth Bowes Lyon, married the Duke of York, second son of George V, who later became George VI. His Queen, Elizabeth, now the much-loved Queen Mother, often stays at her childhood home, and chose it to be the place where Princess Margaret was to be born.

Glamis is supposed to be the centre of a fairy region: there is a tradition that the castle was started on the top of a near-by hill, which was the dwelling-place of the fairies. They would not permit it to be built, scattering by night the stones built up during the day. This association with the supernatural has persisted. Tales of ghostly hauntings, apparitions, strange bangings and fearful sights abound, the events often occurring in the early hours of the morning. The central tower of the castle – its oldest part – is usually the setting for these happenings, and it is this same central tower which is said to contain a hidden room within its walls. But the house remains a very happy home, untroubled by such speculation and giving a warm welcome characteristic of the Bowes Lyon family.

Braemar Castle

Old Mar Castle was built on a mound overlooking the River Dee, where royal castles had stood for over 1000 years. A Pictish King built a fortress on this site to guard the ford over the river, and Angus V had his castle here to receive the remains of St Andrew. Kenneth III also lived here in the tenth century, and soon after came Malcolm III (responsible for the happy ending to Shakespeare's Macbeth) *who was often described as the first real King, because he brought a certain amount of security and peace to the Highlands. All this and much more was history before the Earl of Mar built his castle of Old Mar in 1628. It was supposed to be a hunting-seat, but in reality was built to keep an eye on the Farquharsons of Invercauld, who were becoming extremely powerful. In 1689 the castle was actually burnt out by John Farquharson, the Black Colonel of Inverey, although it was restored in the next century.*

So, is it surprising that spirits of the long, turbulent past should manifest themselves in various ways? Haunting need not be seen but can also be felt and sometimes heard, as this tale, written by The Lady of Invercauld, Mrs Farquharson, will tell.

Opening times:
April–October
Daily 10.00–18.00, except Friday
Tel: (013397) 41219

A tenant of ours at Braemar Castle, as Old Mar is now usually known, told me of his experiences while he was there with his wife, while writing a book.

Each afternoon, I went up to my dressing-room, which, as you know, is next to our double bedroom. Hearing some light footsteps on the landing passage, I called out to my bride, but received no answer. Then again these footsteps, so I called again. When there was no reply, I looked at my watch and was distressed to see how long I had been closeted here, away from my newly-wed wife, whom I had left writing letters in the drawing-room. Of course she must be annoyed with me for my lengthy absence, so I hastily put my papers away and joined her, where she still sat at her desk in the drawing-room. I then chided her for not speaking when she passed my door. Her surprised expression and words saying she had never left her present position annoyed me at first, as I had distinctly heard her both going and coming from our bedroom. However she was so adamant that I called the housekeeper who also insisted that she never climbed 'those rocks', as she described the granite blocks which form the staircase, except to do these rooms in the morning once a day. Whose, then, were the light footsteps?

On a later occasion the same tenant came along to the castle to complete another of his books. It was winter, and he went to his bed after writing for as long as he could, it being a cold night:
'I had not been asleep long when a terrific noise woke me. It sounded like soldiers fighting their way down the stone stairs; bangs of metal against harsh rock. There was no wind, but I finally decided it must be a big brass vase which had somehow fallen the entire way from top to bottom of the stairs, but no, nothing was displaced.' So he remained certain that Braemar is surely haunted.

I have lived in the castle myself since that time, but could never persuade our housekeeper to be there alone, not even during the day, as she was a local, and insisted it was haunted. Then one day when we were in residence in the Castle of Invercauld, I took two guests over to Braemar to visit this much-admired fairy-tale castle. I left the couple outside the curtain-wall, as I wished to open the doors from inside, as the façade looking up from the inside courtyard is fantastic, and there, too, is the rowan tree planted and growing to keep the witches away. As I entered the rear of the castle, I felt someone there, but who? We no longer employed caretakers, so why was I so sure someone was inside? With heart thumping I literally ran to open the front door for our waiting guests. When they had been duly impressed with the courtyard, we all three entered the building, and at once the husband asked: 'Who is here?' Of course I replied no one, and explained that the aged caretakers had found it too isolated for them. But he insisted, 'There is someone here, tell us who.' I repeated that I truly did not know. Together we looked under every bed and in every cupboard and drawer. On every landing – of which there are many as the various rooms are on different levels and lie on either side of a large cylinder stone staircase – Mr X would once again stop and say, 'Please don't go on with this silly game, and just tell us who is here.'

At long last after having searched every room and having looked in every possible hiding-place we returned down the stairs and made our way towards the front entrance, still having seen nothing and not hearing a sound. I decided to keep these two stalwarts with me and leave the castle by the back door. I locked up the front, and silently we went out in single file. Only when we got into my car did Mrs X say 'Thank you', which I took to mean for the tour, but she went on, 'My husband does not believe in the supernatural; I do, and this is the first time he has experienced it.' Her husband now interrupted, 'Oh, stop this nonsense, of course there was someone in the castle, but for some reason of her own, our hostess didn't wish to reveal his whereabouts.' 'However,' his wife continued, 'there *is* someone in the castle, invisible to us; some stray spirit who once belonged to this place.'

I have heard that an ancestor of the Farquharsons, wild, brave, a fabulous horseman, a stealer of wives, a seducer of young women, a killer of anyone who interfered with his freedom, lights his candle and sleeps here some nights. Could it be he, famous in legend for these exploits, the Black Colonel of Inverey?

traquair house

Traquair House, reputed to be the oldest inhabited house in Scotland, is architecturally something of an enigma, reminiscent of a French château, with a style and character of its own spelling out to the observant onlooker a clue here and there to a number of different periods. It is a patchwork of periods both inside and out, with the oldest part dating from the eleventh century. The north end of the main block incorporates the old hunting-lodge, which was used as a royal residence as early as 1100, and the rest of the main block was added as the family fortunes rose, culminating in the rise to power of the first Earl in 1633.

From his time dates the outward appearance of the house as seen today. Since the end of the seventeenth century time has stood still here, for no further alterations were made to the house. Today Traquair is still a family home as it was back in 1492 when James Stuart received it from his father, the Earl of Buchan, who had in turn been granted it by his half-brother James III of Scotland. Before this it had been Crown property; a favourite resort of Scottish royalty who used to hunt in the encircling forests of Traquair and Ettrick.

The story which follows was written by Mr Peter Maxwell Stuart, the twentieth Laird of Traquair.

Opening times:
Easter week, mid April, May–September; other dates by
appointment
Daily (June–September from 10.30) 13.30–17.30
Tel: (01896) 830023

Looking at Traquair in certain lights, especially in the early morning or the gathering dusk, it is difficult to imagine that no ghosts can be said to linger within its ancient walls. Some years ago a worker claimed to have seen an old lady, whose attire closely resembled that of the indomitable Lady Louisa Stuart (she was an earlier owner of Traquair who died in her hundredth year in 1875) walking along her favourite walk by the Quair Burn, but in the house itself no shadow of the past has been seen to flit across a room or appear at the end of a corridor. The family archives reveal no evidence of any ghostly or macabre tales and it is generally accepted that no dark deeds have been perpetrated in the house, which has a warm, friendly and peaceful air. So for ghosts of the past the visitor must rely on his own imagination after going round the house, studying the portraits and reading the letters and some of the many documents which have happily been so well preserved.

But the house has, nevertheless, been at the centre of many exciting events spanning the centuries, and an atmosphere steeped in history envelops the visitor.

Here, for instance, in 1175 William, the Lion of Scotland, flushed after the success of a hard day's hunting, sat down in one of the rooms of Traquair and signed a charter allowing the Bishop of Glasgow to raise the little hamlet on the banks of the River Molendinar to the status of a Royal Borough, having the right to hold its market day on a Thursday. Those who live in Traquair can smile when they recall the saying, 'The Clyde made Glasgow and Glasgow made the Clyde.'

Nearly 100 years earlier Alexander I had visited Traquair, as so many Scottish monarchs were to do after him, and hunted in the surrounding royal forests of Traquair and Ettrick. A charter he signed from Traquair is still in existence along with many others in the house bearing the signatures of kings.

On an autumn afternoon, 9 September 1513, the household of Traquair had leaned out of their windows to watch the archers coming back from Flodden Field with the news that their Laird, James Stuart, was dead, fighting to the last to defend King James, who had also perished, along with most of the nobility of Scotland – 'The Flowers of the Forest'.

69

Fifty-three years later a happier scene took place in the house, for Sir John Stuart, a grandson of James, the first Laird, was host to Mary Queen of Scots and Darnley when they stayed in the house on a hunting expedition to the Tweeddale district. Among the royal company on that occasion was her infant son, James, who on the death of Queen Elizabeth I succeeded to the English throne. His cradle, still preserved at Traquair, is a reminder that its first occupant grew up to unite the Crowns of Scotland and England.

One of the more intriguing features of the interior is the secret staircase leading from a panel concealed behind a cupboard in the Priest's Room down to the King's Room where it connected with another staircase which led out to the back of the house. At a time when Traquair was the only Catholic house of importance in the south of Scotland, the place was frequently searched for priests. The staircase provided a convenient exit for those who wished or were forced to leave the house secretly.

In the 1680s, after the abdication of the Catholic King James II, with feeling running particularly high against Catholics the house was visited by an anti-Royalist mob intent on destroying it. Only the fortitude and resolution of the Dowager Countess of Traquair, who was in the house at the time, prevented a disaster. By allowing the removal of certain religious articles (for burning ceremoniously in Peebles) the insurgents were placated to the extent of complying with the demands of the Countess that they leave behind a precise inventory of the articles they had removed. The inventory can be seen in the Chapel.

During the risings which followed in the next century the chief users of the little staircase were not members of the clergy but Jacobite refugees, supporters or followers of James Francis Stuart and later of his son, Charles Edward Stuart – Bonnie Prince Charlie.

Escapes of one kind or another have always played a leading part in Traquair's history.

It was John Stuart of Traquair, the fourth Laird, who welcomed Mary Queen of Scots to the house in 1566, after personally organising her escape from Holyrood Palace after the murder of her Court favourite, the Italian David Rizzio. Years later he played a similar role in the successful escape she made from the castle at Loch Leven after her defeat at the Battle of Langside.

A hundred years or so passed and another famous figure in Scottish history made an escape, but this time it was from the scene of a battle – Philiphaugh, about fifteen miles from Traquair. It was the Marquis of Montrose, and Traquair House was the first place at which he halted in his flight from the Covenanting army of General Leslie. This time the reception given by the Laird, his kinsman, the first Earl of Traquair, was very different from that given to the Queen of Scots a century before. The great iron-studded door remained bolted and Montrose rode away cursing the Earl for his treachery. Traquair watched hidden from a window, and some time later he welcomed the Covenanters – men who, it is said, marched with their Bibles in their boots. This diplomatic gesture, typical of a man accused of being a 'trimmer', was no doubt responsible for Traquair House not being burned down in revenge for harbouring the rebel Marquis.

A most famous escape associated with Traquair and the family who lived there took place a long way from Scotland – in fact the escape was from the Tower of London. There is little doubt that the ingenious plan of escape was conceived by Winifred, the courageous Countess of Nithsdale. The Countess and her six-year-old daughter Anne spent the Christmas of 1714 at Traquair in the company of her sister-in-law the Countess of Traquair and her family, and had not returned home when the news which she had dreaded was brought to her. The Jacobite Rising aimed at restoring James Francis Edward to the throne had collapsed and among its leaders captured by the English at Preston was her husband, the fifth Earl of Nithsdale. Leaving her daughter at Traquair she returned to her home at Terregles, near Dumfries, and made preparations for the journey to London where she had heard that her husband was imprisoned. In January, accompanied only by her faithful Welsh servant, Cecilia Evans, she took the road via Newcastle, avoiding the shorter Carlisle route because of the danger of encountering Government forces. They then took the stage-coach to York but there had to abandon it because of the severe weather. Continuing the journey by horseback with the snow frequently above the girths of the horses they reached

71

London safely and stayed with the Countess's friend, a Mrs Mills. Here a severe illness, no doubt brought about by the journey, forced the Countess to spend some weeks in bed. By the middle of February she realised that further petitioning of the King would prove useless and was left with no choice but to put into operation her plan for her husband's escape. With the aid of Mrs Mills and Cecilia Evans a suit of lady's clothing was smuggled into the Earl's cell where resigned to his fate he had written his farewell speech which he intended to deliver on the scaffold the next day. (A copy of the speech is preserved in the dining-room.) It was fortunate that in height and build the Earl resembled Mrs Mills. The guards knew the Countess well as she was often in the habit of giving them presents – carefully chosen to ensure that they were not so large as to arouse their suspicions. They were used to her comings and goings, so when two female figures emerged from the cell they were not over careful in their scrutiny and assumed them to be the Countess accompanied by Mrs Mills. The latter was in fact Lord Nithsdale and a carefully prepared plan enabled him to get a passage to France where he landed a few days later, a free man. It would have been easy for the Countess to have left with him but immediately after seeing that he was safely in the care of Evans she returned to his cell in the Tower, carrying on a lively conversation so as to allay still further any suspicions the guards might have, and it was not until the next morning that his escape was discovered.

Traquair was the Countess's destination when she left London secretly soon afterwards, retracing her outward journey but staying only at small inns to avoid being recognised. No doubt the Traquair household thrilled to hear her incredible exploits, but the story does not end there. This remarkable woman returned secretly to her home at Terregles where she put her affairs in order and even buried family documents for safety in the garden. Then once again she left for London but this time accompanied by her daughter, Anne. Incredible as it may seem, the Countess still had hopes of securing an official pardon for her husband in exile and she tried to present a petition for her husband to the King – whom she referred to in letters as the Duke of Hanover! – at one of his official Drawing Room receptions. The King ignored her approach and when she persisted she was rudely brushed aside, incurring a good deal of sympathy from others at Court. The petition was, of course, refused and the King declared that he would have no one speak in her favour. There was no choice for her now but to leave the country and rejoin her husband but her troubles did not end there, as her letters to Traquair reveal. The Nithsdales were plagued by financial problems and the Earl himself, like so many exiled Jacobites, was a spendthrift and gambler. They settled eventually in Rome and the Countess herself became governess to the young Prince Henry, son of James Edward and the younger brother of Charles Edward. She died in 1744.

Of all the stories that have been told and retold about Traquair and the people who lived there, the most famous is the one which has taken its place as one of the more colourful and romantic traditions of Scottish history. The setting is not the house itself but the entrance gates at the end of the Avenue. There are a number of stories about when and why they were closed but to all who are true romantics there is only one explanation.

One day in the late autumn of 1745 the Jacobite army with their Prince, Charles Edward Stuart, at their head set out from Edinburgh bound for England and the road they hoped would end in London. It is probable that the Prince would have visited Traquair, riding over from his temporary headquarters at Kelso on his way either to or from visiting Lord George Murray who, with the western division of his army, was camping near Peebles.

The Prince was anxious to enlist the active participation in the Rising of all leading Jacobites in the area and Traquair certainly was one of these. He himself had the duty of liaison with the English Jacobites and was one of the seven members of the Jacobite association called the 'Concert' whose task it was to organise the movement.

So the Prince arrived at Traquair and was received with all due ceremony by the Earl but, like his ancestor before him in the seventeenth century, the Earl decided to play safe and not commit himself absolutely to the Stuart cause. His brother, John, who succeeded him as the sixth Earl, fought in the campaign but he himself declined to accompany the Jacobite armies. Perhaps, after all, he was following the family tradition of father and son or brother taking opposite sides in war, or political or domestic disputes, so that which ever side won the security of the family estates was ensured. Nevertheless, in a flamboyant gesture of loyalty to the cause he bolted the gates after the royal party had passed through them and placed a curse on any man who opened them before the Stuarts were restored. To this day the gates remain closed and only the two great bears are silent witnesses in stone to the scene that may or may not have taken place there in 1745.

These are just a few of the stories this great house has to tell, there are many more that space does not allow inclusion of here and more still which must belong to the future as work slowly continues piecing together facts gleaned from old documents in the family archives.

Many of its secrets will remain, however, hidden for all time within the bricks, mortar, wood and stone which bind this remarkable building together.

> And what saw ye there
> At the bush aboon Traquair,
> Or what did ye hear that was worth your heed?
> I heard the cushies croon
> Thro' the gowden afternoon
> And the Quair burn singing down the Vale o' Tweed.
> J. Campbell Shairp (1864)

manoerston

Manderston stands just outside the town of Duns, about fifteen miles
west of Berwick upon Tweed. The original house on this site was built
in 1790. In 1864, William – later Sir William – Miller bought the estate.
It was his son Sir James, the second Baronet, who almost entirely
rebuilt and considerably enlarged the house at the beginning of this
century. The architect appointed for this work was John Kinross. He
was strongly influenced in his designs by Kedleston Hall, Derbyshire,
the childhood home of Sir James's wife, which had been designed by
Robert Adam. Manderston as rebuilt by Kinross is a happy mixture of
Classical style blended with Edwardian comfort. Fine plaster ceilings,
the work of French and Italian craftsmen specially brought over for the
task, are a feature of the house. Especially interesting also are the
domestic quarters, complete with their original fittings, and the Marble
Dairy, a veritable palace for the comfort of cows.

Manderston is now the home of Mr Adrian Palmer, great-great-
grandson of Sir William Miller, and Mrs Palmer. The article which
follows was written by Mr Adrian Palmer.

Opening times:
Early May–September; other dates by appointment
Mon (Bank Holiday only), Thurs and Sun
14.00–17.30 (Tues, Wed, Fri, Sat by appointment)
Tel: (01361) 883450; Fax: (01361) 882010

One of the most interesting aspects of Manderston today is that here can be seen very clearly the separate 'upstairs' and 'downstairs' worlds of family and servants, a division normal in large houses right up to the Second World War. The house is fortunate in possessing not only many beautifully decorated reception rooms and bedrooms, but also the original domestic quarters and their furnishings, preserved almost intact.

William Miller made his fortune from trading with Russia in hemp and herrings, and was Honorary British Consul at St Petersburg for sixteen years. On his return he became a Liberal Member of Parliament for Leith and was later elected to represent Berwickshire. For his support, Gladstone made him a Baronet in 1874.

Sir William's second son, James, inherited the estate in 1887 on the death of his father; his elder brother had choked on a cherry-stone at Eton and died. Sir James was very fond of horse-racing, at which he was more fortunate than the average owner, winning a total of £118,000 over a period of twenty years. His horses won numerous races, including in 1890 the Derby with Sainfoin and the Triple Crown (Derby, St Leger and Two Thousand Guineas – won only four times this century) in 1903 with Rocksand, who was sired by Sainfoin.

'Being a good fellow, one of the most wealthy Commoners in the country, and a bachelor, he is a very eligible young man', wrote *Vanity Fair* in 1890. He married three years later, into one of the oldest families in the country. His wife was the Honourable Eveline Curzon, fourth daughter of Lord Scarsdale, of Kedleston Hall in Derbyshire. (It was Eveline's brother who became Viceroy of India.) Sir James wanted above all to impress his father-in-law and at once began improving his estate, by building the boat-house in 1894, the stables in 1895 and the home farm.

The stables were built as a test of Kinross's ability, and are magnificent in their palatial splendour. Built round two courts, the first is entered beneath an arch, flanked with Doric columns and surmounted by a pediment. On the inside of the arch are detailed panels of huntsmen and hounds in high relief. To the left of the courtyard are coach-houses, to the right are loose boxes. The stables cost £20,000 at a time when building was cheap. Without doubt they are the most magnificent club for horses ever built in Scotland and a horse without the right Jockey Club connections would have felt like a rank outsider in it. The roof of selected teak above the stalls is arched like that of a church. The stalls also are made of teak, with polished brass posts. The names of the horses which once occupied them – Mystery, Monarch, Malakoff, etc. – are on marble panels, the tiled feed-troughs are set in teak and all the door fittings and halter-rings are of the finest brass. The harness-room is a polished masterpiece of rich mahogany, with a floor of marble. The exquisite table of brass and Italian marble is of particular note. In case any one should doubt that such splendid surroundings were ever inhabited by horses, it is worth recording that the stables are still used for their original purpose.

Having satisfied Sir James that his work was of sufficiently high standard, Kinross was commissioned to remodel the house, when Sir James returned from the Boer War in 1901.

From the onset of their marriage it had been clear that Sir James and Lady Miller wished to use the house for entertaining their friends, and consequently they required more bedrooms and living accommodation for servants. The house, therefore, was made deeper by demolishing the entrance front and rebuilding it, together with a new wing and service court. On the outside the rather severe style of the old house was kept.

Inside, no expense was spared to ensure that design, workmanship and materials were all of the best quality. 'Upstairs', Kinross worked in the style of Robert Adam to create a new interior which united the old and new parts of the house. His work is so faithful to the spirit of the Georgian period that in some rooms, for example the drawing-room, it is difficult to know whether the decoration is of 1790 or 1901; the visitor may be surprised to learn that in fact all decoration to be seen is of the later date. Perhaps the most splendid room is the ballroom, decorated in Sir James's racing colours of primrose and white. The walls are hung with embossed velvet and the curtains are woven with gold and silver thread. The immaculate condition of the furnishings after seventy-five years is due to the care taken to put the curtains into bags, and coverings on the walls, whenever the room was not in use; rather a contrast to the present-day 'disposable' way of thinking!

'Downstairs', equal care was taken to provide the most up-to-date domestic quarters. The walls of the basement are entirely lined with white tiles, which are easy to keep clean and reflect the light. The most interesting feature of the kitchen is the island cooking range, made by G. Drouet of the Ateliers Briffault in Paris, with an underfloor flue connecting to the chimney, which provides six ovens of different temperatures as well as the hotplate on the top. There was also an open fire for spit-roasting.

The scullery adjoining was for food and vegetable preparation and all washing up. Arrangements for the initial arrival of food were particularly well contrived; tradesmen had a separate door and a separate corridor. When the bell rang, the scullery maid could open the door by way of a lever at the end of the passage to direct the food into whichever of the five larders was appropriate; pastry, raw meat, cooked meat, game/poultry, or fish. His burden delivered, the tradesman could approach the scullery door – no further – to drink a mug of beer from the jar that stood permanently on the table beside it for that purpose.

Also in the basement were the living- and sleeping-quarters for the single menservants and visiting menservants. Female servants slept in the attics, an interesting reflection on the concern to uphold moral standards! This 'great divide' explains also the bell-levers in the bedrooms, marked 'up' (to call a maid from the attic) or 'down' (to call a manservant from the basement).

The housekeeper was responsible for the cleanliness of the house and, therefore, all the housemaids and female staff came under her command. At Manderston in 1905 there were three laundry maids, six housemaids, three scullery maids, and the cook. The housekeeper was also responsible for the care of the extensive, elaborate and expensive china services, which were kept in cupboards in her room. The household linen was kept in the adjacent linen store, also under strict supervision.

Outside can be found the Marble Dairy, which rivals the stables in the magnificence of its accommodation for non-humans. The boss in the centre of the roof shows a milkmaid milking. At Sir James's insistence, the first one put there was taken down and recarved because the girl was on the wrong side of the cow; such was the attention to detail. It weighs literally half a ton. One of the most skilful architectural features of the room, however, is one of the least noticed: the vaulting over the entrance door which is set at an angle from the walls of the room, making the corner an especially awkward shape. The whole was created by Italian and French craftsmen. It is a poem in the marbles of seven different countries and its lovely groined roof was the last word in that poem. The doors of this bijou are of solid teak – not a nail in them. The remainder of the dairy looks as if it had been designed for sacred cows. It is in the form of an ancient Roman cloister with a fountain in the centre. A dainty spiral stair leads up to a turret room completely panelled in oak, where again no nails have been used. There, the chatelaine of Manderston could sip tea from priceless china – it is still there – and enjoy the commanding view.

To visit Manderston is to step back for a brief period to the luxury and opulence of the Edwardian era, when comfort was the prime goal in design and excellence of workmanship encouraged and admired. But it was the domestic staff who ensured the smooth running of the household, and it is rare to find such care being lavished on their quarters. Sir James Miller was certainly more enlightened than many of his contemporaries in this respect, and his efforts must have been as much appreciated then, by the people working there, as they are today by visitors.

floors castle

Floors Castle stands just outside Kelso in the Borders Region and is the seat of the Duke of Roxburghe, head of the Innes Ker family. It was begun in 1721, to a design by William Adam. But it was the sixth Duke who was responsible for the castle as it appears today. It was he who, in 1841, commissioned William Playfair, architect of the National Gallery in Edinburgh among other well-known buildings, to enlarge and redesign Floors. He added extensive wings to either side of the main building and ornamented the roofs with turrets, pinnacles and battlements to create a most exotic skyline. Much of the interior of the castle was remodelled at the beginning of this century by the eighth Duchess.

Floors is now the home of the tenth Duke and Duchess of Roxburghe.

Opening times:
April–June, September
Sun–Thurs 10.30–17.30
July–August
Daily 10.30–17.30
October
Sun and Wed 10.30–16.30)
Tel: (01573) 223333; Fax: (01573) 226056

Floors Castle occupies one of the most beautiful sites in Scotland, overlooking the River Tweed just outside the town of Kelso. However, it was not always the land of Oberon and Titania so lyrically described by Sir Walter Scott, but more the land of raid and counter-raid between the Scots and the English. Roxburgh Castle, known as Marchmont, which lies immediately above the junction of the Rivers Tweed and Teviot and faces Floors Castle, was the strongest fortress on the entire Border.

Edward I first captured Roxburgh Castle from the Scots and ordered Mary, sister of Robert the Bruce, to be suspended from the castle walls in a cage for five years; she miraculously survived this horrific torture. In 1313, three years after Mary's ordeal, the castle fell to the Scots led by Sir James Douglas only for it to be recaptured by Edward III of England from Edward Baliol. The castle remained in English hands for the next century, and it was not until 1460 that it was once again taken by the Scots, but at the cost of James II of Scotland losing his life in the attempt.

Artillery had only been introduced to Scotland at the end of the fourteenth century and it was James II who started to use cannon as the normal instrument of siege. His wife, Mary de Guelders, gave him, as part of her dowry, guns manufactured in the Low Countries. The siege of Roxburgh Castle began on Sunday, 3 August 1460, and naturally James employed his newly acquired artillery. He stood too close to one of the cannon, known as 'The Lion', it exploded, either from being overloaded or from a weakness in its design and he was killed. On hearing the news of his death, Mary travelled to Roxburgh with the infant James III, then eight years old, and urged the Scots to victory. The Scots carried the castle by storm and, to prevent the English from being tempted to return, razed it to the ground.

Not until the reign of Henry VIII did the reconstruction of Roxburgh Castle begin, and as a military work this new fortalice had but a short life. Fulfilling the terms of the peace treaty concluded between England and France in 1550, Edward VI evacuated Scotland and demolished Roxburgh Castle, and in 1553 Mary Queen of Scots, granted 'terras et baronium de Auld Roxburgh cum castro, castri loco' to Sir Walter Ker of Cessford and Roxburgh, grandfather of the first Earl of Roxburghe.

Floors Castle looks over the same countryside, but has never experienced the feuding of earlier times. However, there is a reminder of these times; in the park between Floors and the River Tweed there stands a holly tree planted to commemorate the place where James II was killed while besieging Roxburgh Castle.

Dalmeny house

Dalmeny House stands on a wide grassy sward on the shores of the Firth of Forth between the coasts of Fife and Edinburgh and looking far out to the open North Sea. Beside and behind the house are fine trees and sheep crop the grass and great flocks of sea birds – gulls, dunlin and oystercatchers – flash in the sun as they fly in to land on the muddy sands exposed by the low tide. One can follow the coastal footpath for four miles between Cramond and South Queensferry, finding rocky pools and golden beaches, emerging from deep peaceful woodland to walk across the great open space in front of the house. Yet only a mile away is the busy A9 and it is just eight miles to the centre of Edinburgh. The article which follows was written by the Countess of Rosebery.

Opening times:
May–September; other dates by appointment
Sun 13.00–17.30, Mon and Tues 12.00–17.30
Tel: (0131) 331 1888; Fax: (0131) 331 1788

The Earls of Rosebery have lived at Dalmeny for 300 years. The present house was built in 1815, but the original house on the estate, twelfth-century Barnbougle Castle, was built by the Mowbray family on a rocky point a quarter of a mile away. Originally Knights Templar, the Mowbrays became noted for 'brawling and smuggling', sailing contraband right into the cellars of their castle. Sir Roger de Mowbray fought in the Crusades and there is a story that on the very night that he was killed in Palestine, fighting the Saracens, his hound howled all night long on a headland near the castle. Since then, it is said, the 'ghost' hound is heard to howl on the night the Laird of Barnbougle dies. The headland, Hound Point, has given its name to the oil export terminal which can be seen from the Forth Bridge.

The father of the first Earl of Rosebery, Sir Archibald Primrose, bought Barnbougle for his son in 1662. Sir Archibald was a Royalist lawyer, Clerk to the Privy Council under Charles I, and at the Restoration Charles II made him Lord Clerk Register. His son, the first Earl, opposed James II's policies, and served abroad in the army, returning as Gentleman of the Bedchamber to George I.

The second Earl was a spendthrift and a profligate. The castle fell into disrepair and his sons went to London, where the elder, Lord Dalmeny, met and fell in love with a certain Kitty Canham. Travelling under an assumed name, he took her abroad. He married her and while living in Verona she died. On her deathbed she confessed to bigamy. She was the wife of a vicar in Essex and her dying wish was to be buried at her old home. The desolate Lord Dalmeny travelled back with the embalmed body and on the crossing to Harwich he was seized by customs men who suspected him of smuggling contraband in the coffin and demanded that it be opened. The body was discovered, and as Lord Dalmeny still refused to give his name, the coffin was placed in a church near Colchester while inquiries were made, he maintaining his vigil beside it. Curious locals crowded in, and one of them suddenly recognised Kitty Canham as the wife of the Vicar of near-by Thorpe-le-Soken. The Vicar was sent for and arrived, brandishing his sword, to fight the man who had stolen his wife – but the two were reconciled, and Kitty Canham went to her grave followed by two sorrowing husbands.

Lord Dalmeny returned home, and tried to busy himself with plans for the improvement of the family lands, but he died soon afterwards and his younger brother, Neil, succeeded their father in 1755 as the third Earl of Rosebery.

The third Lord Rosebery was still living in the cold and damp cramped twelfth-century castle a hundred years after Barnbougle had been bought for his grandfather, the first Earl. Family tradition has it that when his family complained about the castle he said, 'What was good enough for my grandfather should be good enough for my grandson' until one day a wave crashed into the dining-room window and extinguished the candles. In 1774, Lord Rosebery, a widower, was courting a new wife, and he invited Robert Adam, whom he had met in Italy on the Grand Tour, to design improvements to his home. Adam's magnificent plan, incorporating a triangular courtyard, huge banqueting hall and a semicircular harbour, was too impractical, and the new Lady Rosebery had to make do with bringing up their children in the old castle.

This Earl of Rosebery was very vain and liked no one to know he had gone bald when quite young. He had wigs of three different lengths, and wore them in rotation, travelling to Edinburgh for a 'haircut' in the long wig, with the short one in his pocket.

As a young man in London Lord Rosebery had developed a great liking for facts and figures and his Grand Tour journals barely mention visits he made, but dwell in great detail on reports of shipping and trade, travelling expenses, and how far he travelled each day.

He lived to be eighty-seven in his sea-girt castle, looking through his telescope, and making notes in his diary about the shipping, the weather, the trees, the crops and farm, and the declining distance his old dog Rover would walk before demanding to be put in the carriage.

He grumbled about his son's plans to build a new house on various unsuitable sites, and about his flighty daughter-in-law. He died in 1814, leaving a well-farmed estate, and a dilapidated castle to his son. He was right about his daughter-in-law, for she ran away the following year. She fell in love with her dead sister's husband, and eloped with him in a rowing-boat to Cramond, and thence abroad. Perhaps the cold little castle was the last straw. Lord Rosebery divorced her, and in 1815 he commissioned William Wilkins to build him a new house – the present Dalmeny House. Wilkins's design was the first 'Tudor Gothic' house in Scotland and was revolutionary in the convenience of its domestic arrangements. In 1818 Lord Rosebery married again and brought his new wife to his new house, leaving Barnbougle Castle to the rooks and the ivy. His son, Lord Dalmeny, predeceased him and he was succeeded by his grandson as fifth Earl.

The fifth Earl of Rosebery was a scholar, historian and book-collector from childhood. An outstanding figure among his contemporaries he was renowned as an orator. He wrote books on the lives of the great statesmen, Pitt, Chatham, Churchill and Napoleon. He entered politics as a Liberal, becoming Foreign Secretary and then Prime Minister on Gladstone's resignation in 1894.

He married Hannah, only child of Baron Meyer de Rothschild who had built Mentmore Towers in Buckinghamshire to house his fabulous collection of paintings, furniture and other works of art.

In 1881, at the request of the Commissioners of Northern Lights, instead of demolishing it as a dangerous ruin Lord Rosebery rebuilt the crumbling Barnbougle Castle as a private sanctuary and refuge from his family and friends. He often spent the night there, in a simple iron bed, in a little tower room overlooking the sea. He wrote his speeches and his books in the quiet book-lined study, and his son remembered, as a child, seeing his father walking back, wrapped in a cloak, to join the family for dinner.

Lord Rosebery was particularly interested in the life of Napoleon, and formed a fascinating collection of books, paintings, furniture and other objects associated with the Emperor. This collection, and the finest of the French eighteenth-century furniture, porcelain and tapestries collected by Baron Meyer de Rothschild at Mentmore, are now at Dalmeny and can be seen by visitors to the house.

The sixth Earl was a noted sportsman who not only captained Surrey, but also played polo, was a superb shot and was M.F.H. of the Whaddon Chase. His most widely known interest was, however, the turf. At his stud at Mentmore he owned and bred two Derby winners: Blue Peter in 1939 and Ocean Swell in 1944.

He had a distinguished career in the First World War, being

awarded the D.S.O. and the M.C. He served on many public bodies and was Regional Commissioner for Scotland during the Second World War. He died in 1974, aged ninety-two.

The present Lord Rosebery, the seventh Earl, lives in Dalmeny House and farms the estate, he takes particular interest in his beautiful trees and plans and plants for his grandchildren.

Lauriston castle

Lauriston Castle stands within the boundaries of the City of Edinburgh. The first record of Lauriston is as a farm belonging to the Crown at the end of the thirteenth century. It was not until about 1590 that the tower-house, the oldest part of the present structure, was built by Sir Archibald Napier. The tower-house stood alone till 1827, when Thomas Allan employed William Burn to create a Jacobean-style mansion with the tower-house as a basis. Fifty years later a first-floor library was added above a single-storey wing designed by Burn. Since then, the house has remained almost unchanged, a microcosm of life in late Victorian and Edwardian times. This is no accident but is in strict accordance with the wishes of the last owners, Mr and Mrs W. R. Reid, who left the castle to the nation on the condition that it would be maintained much as it was in their lifetimes. Mrs Reid outlived her collector-husband by seven years and since her death in 1926 Lauriston has been administered as a trust by the City of Edinburgh. Like some rare insect entombed in amber, the castle will remain for ever a preserved relic of the self-assured and prosperous Edwardian era.

The story which follows was written by Mr Herbert Coutts, City Curator for the City of Edinburgh Museums and Art Galleries.

In trust by the City of Edinburgh

Opening times:
April–October
Daily 11.00–17.00, except Friday
November–March
Sat and Sun 14.00–16.00

The earliest known reference to the lands of Lauriston occurs in the Exchequer Rolls of 1290, from which it is clear that at that time they belonged to the Crown. Later (by the middle of the fifteenth century) the estate came into the hands of the family of Laurenstoun of that Ilk. However, the oldest structural element in the present castle, a late-sixteenth-century tower-house which forms its south-west corner, is attributed to Sir Archibald Napier of Edinbellie and Merchiston. Sir Archibald married twice and by his first wife was the father of John Napier, the inventor of logarithms, who ultimately inherited Merchiston. It was after his second marriage to Elizabeth Mowbray that he purchased Lauriston and constructed there a sturdy fortalice, very much a reflection of the troubled age in which it was erected. Lauriston's builder was widely believed to be a wizard, as also was his famous son, John, the 'Marvellous Merchiston'. One of the public offices that Sir Archibald held for a time was that of Master of the Cunzie-House or Mint, and metallurgical experiments which he carried out added fuel to the popular belief in his necromantic skills. As a young man during the troubled reign of Mary Queen of Scots he became widely known as a seer when, as the Queen's own Secretary recorded, 'The Laird of Markyston, who had the reputation of being a great wizard, made bets with several persons to the amount of five hundred crowns, that by the 5th of May Her Majesty would be out of Lochleven.' Mary escaped on the 2nd of May 1568.

An attractive feature of the tower are two large angle turrets that enhance its southern corners. The story of a forbidden love-affair has long been associated with the upper centre window in the western turret and its unusual projecting sill. Legend has it that it was by placing a lantern or beacon on this semicircular ledge that Janet Lauriston communicated with her lover James Mowbray of near-by Barnbougle Castle, against the express wishes of her father. The two lovers eventually married but the credibility of the story is dented somewhat by the fact that all this took place more than half a century before the tower was built. Perhaps there was another pair of lovers whose names have been forgotten, or perhaps the 'beacon stone' was used for the more prosaic purpose of signalling simultaneously to the castles at Merchiston and Barnbougle – Sir Archibald's wife was the daughter of Robert Mowbray of Barnbougle.

Inside the tower-house is a secret room, 'the prophet's chamber', which is reached by swinging out an innocent-looking window-shutter in the Oak Room, formerly the hall of the early castle. This reveals a hidden stairway, claimed to be the narrowest in Scotland, leading to a small chamber, roofed and floored with stone and with a raised stone platform, and lit by a tiny window. The chamber is equipped with a listening aperture that doubles as a spyhole, through which, before the lowering of the Oak Room ceiling in the nineteenth century, it would have been possible to hear, and to a more limited extent see, what went on in the castle's principal apartment. No accurate information is available as to why Sir Archibald Napier should require such a room, but speculation abounds. A hiding-place is one possibility; another is that Sir Archibald, who was a prominent figure of his day, may have found it useful to have a servant overhear the conversations of powerful visitors to Lauriston when, on some pretext, he absented himself from the hall for a period – we will never know!

On Sir Archibald's death in 1608 Lauriston came into the possession of his eldest son by his second marriage, Alexander Napier. A tumultuous spirit in his youth, when fifteen years old Alexander took part in a 'sit-in' at Edinburgh High School, which makes today's examples of student unrest look tame by comparison. In the company of several fellow students, he seized the school and refused to give it up in the face of requests from both the schoolmaster and the Provost and magistrates of Edinburgh. At length the civic authorities were, in the words of the contemporary Burgh Records, '. . . compellit to ding in peices ane of the durris thairof and win the same be force, at the quhilk time the said scholers wes fund with pistols, swords, halberts and uther wawpouns and airmour, aganis all guid ordour and lawes, and to the evill exampill of utheris.' Because most of the offending youths were the sons of noblemen they escaped serious punishment.

Four years later, Alexander found himself in even more serious trouble when, accompanied by his nephew Archibald, he attacked

John Hepburne, servant of the Master of Elphingstoun, on the stairhead of the Edinburgh Tolbooth. From a description of the incident in the Register of the Privy Council it would appear that Alexander had 'come upon him [Hepburne] and with great force and violence dang him forward over the stairhead, to the grit hazard and perell of his lyfe and breking of his bones.' The gravity of the offence was exacerbated by the fact that the Court of Session was sitting in the Tolbooth at the time, as the Scots Parliament had recently ordained the penalty of death for anyone found guilty of striking or hurting another in the outer Tolbooth during Session sittings. Fortunately for Napier, when the King and Council considered the charge it was not upheld because the Master of Elphingstoun was unable to provide all the necessary proof. Perhaps as a precaution against the worst, Alexander had failed to appear at the hearing, and for this reason was denounced as a rebel and his father was ordered to produce him at a later meeting of the Privy Council.

Of course, these were violent times and incidents of this sort were commonplace. So it is no great surprise to find that in maturity Alexander Napier was knighted, gave good service to his country when filling a number of public offices, and was eventually made a Lord of Session (a judge in Scotland's Supreme Civil Court), taking the title Lord Lauriston. He is known to have been interested in astrology, a reminder of which is his 'celestial theme' or horoscope (possibly calculated by his brother John) carved into a stone plaque, now set into the wall of the tower.

Towards the end of the seventeenth century Lauriston was inherited by another reckless spirit, the most renowned of its long line of owners – John Law. Law's father, William, an Edinburgh goldsmith and banker, had purchased Lauriston in June 1683 but may never have lived there as he died not long after. John, William's eldest surviving son, was then twelve years of age. He was educated at the Edinburgh High School and at Eaglesham. Fond of sport, he is reputed to have excelled at tennis. Law was so fastidious with regard to his attire that he was given the sobriquets 'Beau Law' and 'Jessamy John'.

While still young he made for London, where he quickly assumed the life-style of a dissipated man of fashion, soon accumulating large debts. To clear them Law sold his interest in Lauriston to his mother in 1693. In the following year he had a serious difference with another London dandy, Edward Wilson, the son of a Leicestershire squire, which resulted in a duel with swords in Bloomsbury Square and Wilson's death. Law was apprehended, being charged, with singular precision, that 'of his malice aforethought and assault premeditated, [he] made an assault upon Edward Wilson with a certain sword made of iron and steel of the value of five shillings with which he inflicted one mortal wound of the breadth of two inches, and of the depth of five inches, of which mortal wound the said Edward Wilson then and there instantly died.' Not surprisingly, he was found guilty but was saved from death by powerful friends who intervened to obtain a pardon. The reprieve might have been short-lived as his victim's brother immediately lodged an appeal to the Court of the King's Bench, whereupon Law was taken into custody again. Determined not to risk the possibility of the appeal being upheld, he escaped and fled to the Continent. A not too flattering description of the escapee was included in a notice offering a reward for his recapture which appeared in the *London Gazette* of 7 January 1695: 'Captain John Lawe, a Scotchman, lately a prisoner in the King's Bench for Murther, aged 26, a very tall, black, lean man, well shaped, above six foot high, large pock holes in his face, big high nosed, speaks broad and loud. . . .'

In virtual exile, he returned to a youthful interest in finance (perhaps a result of his father's influence) by studying Dutch banking methods. He visited many European capitals, and by speculation and skill at gambling began to amass a large fortune. When his mother died in 1707 he once again inherited Lauriston. As his personal fortune grew so did his reputation for financial acumen. In 1716 he received permission from the Duc d'Orleans, Regent of France, to establish a private bank in Paris. Law's policy of issuing paper money at fixed values at a period when the country's coinage was constantly fluctuating in value, and of freely lending money at low interest rates, had an immediate beneficial effect on the French economy, financially exhausted following the long wars of Louis XIV's reign.

His reputation assured by the success of his bank, in 1717 he next suggested the formation of a trading company to develop and exploit French territories along the Mississippi – the so-called 'Mississippi Scheme'. The apparent success of Law's company led to it being given similar trading rights in regard to the French colonies in Senegal, East India, China and Africa. Now called the 'Compagnie des Indes', it was soon controlling France's entire foreign trade outside Europe. At the height of its power, Law's company also undertook the collection and management of taxation revenues and assumed responsibility for the French National Debt.

These developments produced an upsurge in French prosperity and confidence, with Law being seen as the saviour of the nation. He had become the most important figure in France after the Regent and proved to be an able and reforming administrator. It is told of him that he was visited in Paris by the Duke of Argyll who found the ante-rooms of his residence crowded with the most important people in France waiting impatiently for an audience. Coming from Law's country of origin the Duke was given precedence, but upon being ushered into the great man's chamber he found him writing at his desk. When the Duke asked him what important item of State business had detained him from seeing the assembled French nobility, he replied that he had been writing a letter to his gardener at Lauriston with regard to the planting of cabbages!

In 1720 Law was made Comptroller-General of the Finances of France, in effect its Prime Minister. But this ultimate triumph was short-lived as frenzied speculation in his company's shares led to an inevitable reaction, with the consequence that the company crashed. His life in danger, Law was obliged to leave France while all his property, in which he had invested his fortune, was confiscated. He returned to London in 1721, living there for four years (it is not known if he visited Lauriston during this period), before settling in Venice, where he died in relative poverty in 1729. Lauriston now passed to John's brother William, remaining in the possession of his heirs for almost a century. It has been suggested that during the 140 years that the Laws owned Lauriston no member of the family may ever have resided there.

It was during the nineteenth century that Lauriston was transformed from an austere fortified tower into a gracious country mansion. Most of this was achieved by Thomas Allan – banker, newspaper-proprietor and amateur mineralogist (giving his name to the mineral Allanite) – who purchased the castle in 1823. Allan employed the well-known Edinburgh architect William Burn to design a large extension to the castle in the fashionable English Jacobean style. Fortunately, few alterations were made to the tower though that might not have been the case if the architect had had his way. Sir Walter Scott noted in his Journal that on 3 December 1827 he 'went with Tom Allan to see his building at Lauriston, where he has displayed good taste – supporting instead of tearing down or destroying the old château, which once belonged to the famous Mississippi Law. The additions are in very good taste, and will make a most comfortable house. Mr. Burn, architect, would fain have had the old house pulled down, which I wonder at in him, though it would have been the practice of most of his brethren.' Later in the century Thomas Macknight Crawfurd added a library at the east end of the house.

In 1902 the property was purchased for the last time, by William Robert Reid, the proprietor of a successful Edinburgh firm of cabinet-makers. He took particular pleasure in filling Lauriston with his extensive collection of period furniture, prints and *objets d'art*. Childless, Mr and Mrs Reid decided to leave Lauriston, its collection and grounds to the nation, 'for the use of the public in all time coming, with a view to the education of public taste'. Also the contents of Mr Reid's library were gifted to the National Library of Scotland.

Unusually for a building of such antiquity, no ghost stories have previously appeared in print in connection with Lauriston. Thus, it was an especially welcome 'find' when my attention was drawn to a manuscript account of a Lauriston Castle ghost held by the Edinburgh Room of Edinburgh Central Library. This was compiled by Captain A. C. Crawfurd, nephew of Thomas Macknight Crawfurd who owned the castle from 1871 to 1902. According to Captain Crawfurd the Lauriston Castle ghost takes the form of a shuffling figure in slippers (thought to be the uneasy spirit of a former butler), which has been frequently heard, though never seen, approaching a small isolated room, to which access is obtained by a narrow winding passage.

In support of the legend he quotes a story told to him in October 1931 by Mr John Fairley, a personal friend of the Reids and the first Curator of the Castle. Crawfurd is careful to point out that Fairley, a cautious and intelligent middle-aged man, had indicated that he did not believe in ghosts. Although he occupied a detached house specially built for the castle curator, when the Lauriston house-keeper was away he invariably slept in the castle. Towards the end of September 1931 Fairley had occasion to spend the night in the room in question.

'Nothing disturbed his slumbers until after midnight, when he was awakened by the sound of someone approaching his room from along the passage, and he distinctly heard the curious shuffling sound of feet moving in loose slippers. On reaching the right-angle turning, he particularly noticed there was a pause. He sat up in bed and at the moment he thought the apparition was about to enter the room, he switched on a small electric torch which he always placed under his pillow. He saw nothing, and heard nothing further, and before long he was fast asleep. His slumbers were again disturbed by the most appalling crash he had ever heard in his life as if a bomb had struck the roof and exploded close to his bedside. He lay perfectly still for a few minutes, thinking over the position, and wondering what next would occur, but all was again silent in the Castle, and no movement anywhere. He again switched on his torch and surveyed the room.

'What had happened was this: a large heavy picture, framed in glass, which had been hanging over his washing stand, close beside his bed, had fallen upon the glass utensils below, causing the crash which had suddenly awakened him. He again turned over and went to sleep and nothing more occurred.'

When Crawfurd asked Fairley if he had connected the approach of the ghost with the subsequent fall of the picture, he (ever sensible) replied that he did not and that the picture probably fell simply because the nail by which it was attached to the wall had rusted from old age. I wonder. . . .

cameron house

Cameron House, beautifully situated on the shores of Loch Lomond, has been the home of the Smollett family since James Smollett bought the Cameron Estates in 1763. Previously, the Smolletts had lived at the Place of Bonhill. A stone keep, with many underground passages stretching out to the loch and the hillside above, had stood at Cameron as long ago as the fourteenth century, and by the eighteenth century this had been fashioned into a fine house. Extensive alterations were made in 1806, while in 1865, after a fire, the house was rebuilt and considerably enlarged by Patrick Smollett.

Over the centuries the house, partly because of its situation on an important route to the Highlands, has been visited by many notable people including Dr Johnson, who stayed here with Boswell in 1772 and remarked, 'We have had more solid talk here than any other place.'

Open only as a hotel and residential time-share complex
Tel: (01389) 755565

Loch Lomond has, according to local legend, exercised the power of life and death over the head of the Smollett household. The story has been passed down over the centuries that whenever the loch freezes over completely, the head of the household will die. Certainly, in past centuries when the qualification has been fulfilled, a Smollett has died – the last time that this occurred was in 1860. But Loch Lomond only freezes over completely once every fifty years, and sceptics might well argue that the deaths have more probably been due to a combination of old age and, presumably, very intense cold which had to be withstood without the modern benefits of efficient heating. The present owner, Mr Patrick Telfer Smollett, survived the last complete freeze-over quite unscathed, despite having tempted fate somewhat by driving a car right over the frozen loch!

But within the house is a room in which events have occurred which defy such prosaic explanation. Objects have been 'seen' in this room, which in fact do not exist, despite their apparent solidity. On one occasion, a little boy saw a most vivid image of a doll's house, and rushed, in the way of all small boys, to tell his mother and nurse, who expressed polite, if disbelieving, astonishment. But the feigned surprise turned to genuine amazement when, two months later, the little boy was given a doll's house for Christmas and, as soon as he saw it, said, 'But that's the doll's house I saw – how did you know what it was like?' In order to prevent people anticipating apparitions and, therefore, convincing themselves that they have seen something strange, the room is never identified to strangers, but still the ghostly objects appear and defy rational explanation.

The most frightening legend which the Lairds hand down is associated not with the present family home, but with the Place of Bonhill, the old family mansion which was pulled down in 1950. It was a mysterious old house, medieval in origin, and, as with many historic houses, there was a secret passage. This dark and gloomy tunnel led down from a hidden entrance behind the drawing-room fireplace, and reputedly connected with an escape route having its exit on the banks of the River Leven. One day in 1785 a piper was sent down this tunnel to frighten away the rats which swarmed in their dozens in the dark recesses of the passageway. The piper vanished without trace and was never seen again – but the rats still scratched and scampered. For many generations later, in the stillness of the night could be heard a faint and musical piping, deep within the walls.

Drumlanrig castle

Drumlanrig Castle, home of the Dukes of Buccleuch and Queensberry, is an ancient Douglas stronghold which lies about fifteen miles north-west of Dumfries. It was originally founded in the fourteenth century, on a site which dominated the lovely Nith Valley. Its name denotes its setting: on a hill (Drum) *at the end of a long* (lang) *ridge* (rig). *The existing castle was built of pale pink sandstone between 1679 and 1690 for the first Duke of Queensberry. His son played a significant part in the Act of Union between England and Scotland in 1707. In 1745 it was occupied by Prince Charles Edward.*

Today, the castle is the home of the ninth Duke of Buccleuch and eleventh Duke of Queensberry, and it houses remarkable collections of furniture, relics of Bonnie Prince Charlie and, most outstanding of all, art treasures, including Rembrandt's masterpiece An Old Woman Reading. *Surrounding the castle is a beautiful park in which stands the ruined Tibber's Castle, destroyed by Bruce in 1311.*

The story which follows was written by Lorna MacEchern, Private Secretary to His Grace The Duke of Buccleuch and Queensberry.

Opening times:
Early May – late August
Daily, except Thurs 11.00–17.00, Sun 13.00–17.00
Grounds and Adventure Woodland:
Early May – late September
Tel: (01848) 331682 (24-hour answering service);
Country Park (01848) 331555

Distinguished guests have been welcomed from Mary Queen of Scots and King James VI and I, whose portraits still hang in the house, to Astronaut Neil Armstrong (the Red Oak he planted can be seen in the garden), while less welcome visitors to Drumlanrig were the English in 1547 who, 'manifest thieves and traitors', stole nearly 500 cattle from Sir James Douglas; they were drawn to the gallows (the Gallows Flat is in the park near the castle), hanged and quartered.

Prince Charles Edward Stuart was another uninvited guest who in December 1745, retreating from his defeat at Derby, demanded a night's lodging for himself and about 2000 men. Straw was laid in rooms where the soldiers slept, while Bonnie Prince Charlie occupied the Duke of Queensberry's bedroom. The Highlanders left the castle in a 'sad pickle', having killed about forty sheep in the vestibule and kept their horses under the Gallery; they destroyed all the spirits and most of the wine, broke chairs and tables, melted down pewter, carried away linen and other items, and badly damaged a painting of King William III. This picture has been restored, but the marks of the Jacobites' swords can still be seen by today's visitors to Drumlanrig, as can the room and bed where the Prince slept, together with interesting Jacobite relics and portraits.

James Fergusson, the Duke's Chamberlain, managed to save some things of value and the best of the bed- and table-linen (some small pieces dated 1721 are still in the linen cupboard) before he prudently retired to his own home of Craigdarroch, and the Charter Room was untouched by the soldiers as the castle servants assured them that it contained nothing but papers.

Ill luck again struck Drumlanrig later in the century, when both sons of Charles, third Duke of Queensberry, died young, fulfilling – the superstitious might say – the prophecy of Thomas the Rhymer:

> When the Marr Burn runs where man never saw
> The House of the Hassock is near a fa'.

Drumlanrig Castle was also known as the 'House of the Hassock'. Kitty, wife of the third Duke, had diverted the course of the Marr Burn, to make a fountain and cascade to the south of the house.

On Duke Charles's death, without heirs, the Estate passed to a cousin, William, fourth Duke of Queensberry, who brought devastation to the lands of Drumlanrig by the complete neglect of his Scottish home which, during his thirty-two years as Duke, he seldom visited, and then only to reap a financial harvest from its fine trees and tenanted farms, to spend on his dissolute London life.

After his death, however, when the Queensberry title and lands came, by inheritance, to the Duke of Buccleuch, the estate prospered as a result of careful management by generations of Dukes of Buccleuch and Queensberry, until today Drumlanrig is the nucleus of a thriving rural estate, making a striking contribution to the cultural and agricultural life of the country.

The castle is strangely unchanged and timeless. Although the dungeons are now muniment rooms, the huge old kitchen – was it here that those slaughtered sheep were cooked for the Young Chevalier? – is now a delightful tea-room for visiting tourists; Duchess Kitty's cascade has gone although her Wishing Well remains, and the Marr Burn happily follows its original course through well-tended woodlands of great beauty; the great iron yetts still swing sweetly on their hinges – relics of the earlier castle; the barn owls still snore in the turrets; swifts scream round the towers and nest in the centuries-old stonework; and if there are ghosts, they are friendly ones, who return not to haunt their successors, but to revisit a happy home.

pitcaple castle

Pitcaple Castle stands near the village of Pitcaple, about twenty miles north-west of Aberdeen. The lands of 'Pethapil', as it was then called, were granted to David Leslie in 1457 by a Charter bearing the seal of James II. This can still be seen at the castle. However, another Charter shows that the 'Thane's Tower' was probably in existence in 1411. To this tower was added a keep and a staircase tower, creating a Z-plan castle.

In 1511 King James IV granted a Charter making Pitcaple a 'free Barony', so today Margaret Burges-Lumsden holds the title of Baroness of Pitcaple.

After 300 years of Leslie ownership, the castle passed by marriage to the Lumsdens.

One of the many fascinating incidents in the castle's history occurred in 1650 when the Marquis of Montrose, who had fought many successful battles for Charles I, and then gone into exile when Charles was executed, returned to Scotland. His ill-trained army was defeated at Carbisdale. Sorely wounded, he escaped from the final slaughter but was betrayed for a ransom. This event is related in one of the following stories.

In the late eighteenth century the castle fell into disrepair but was restored in the next century by Hugh Lumsden. He replaced the turret tops with curved profiles, and added on the stately mansion.

The stories which follow were written by Captain Patrick Burges-Lumsden.

Now closed to the public.

The Robin Messengers

In the mid seventeenth century there was an old woman, who lived near Pitcaple Castle, called the 'Guid wifee of Glack' and she was reputed to have the power of second sight, which meant that she was able to foretell future events and to warn if a death was imminent in any household.

The Laird of Pitcaple at this time was Sir John Leslie, and his wife Agnes Ramsay of Balmayne was much liked by the countryfolk to whom she was very kind and generous.

One day when she met up with this 'Guid wifee of Glack', the latter said to her:

'If a robin redbreast in your home appear
It is a warning you should heed and fear
He brings you tidings that a loved one of your ain
Will journey forth and ne'er come back again.'

An army of Covenanters had recently passed by Pitcaple, heading towards Inverness and the north, for news was filtering through that the famous Royalist General, the Marquis of Montrose, had returned from his self-imposed exile and was raising an army to win back the throne for Prince Charles, whose father King Charles I had been beheaded in Whitehall the previous year by the Cromwellians.

Sir John Leslie had ridden off, probably to try and join up with Montrose's army, so Lady Leslie was in charge of the castle, but without any able-bodied men to defend it.

Then one evening, on looking westward from one of the topmost windows, Agnes Leslie spied a small cavalcade of horses approaching, and in their midst, sitting astride a decrepit garron pony, was a figure with one of his arms strapped across his chest with what appeared to be crude bandages, and his feet anchored beneath the animal's belly with ropes of hay, so that he could not leap off and escape from what were obviously his captors.

The party of horsemen rode up to the drawbridge that gave entry to the castle over its surrounding moat but kept intruders from bursting in without warning. Their leader demanded that they be admitted so that they could shelter for the night. Riding over the drawbridge, which had been lowered, and in through the gateway of the outer curtain-wall, the weary figure on the pony was released, and Lady Leslie, standing in the low entrance doorway, had to stifle her cry of distress when she saw that the soldierly figure was her cousin James Graham, Marquis of Montrose. How, she wondered, could he be a captive, he who in the previous ten years had won so many battles against the odds, always with inferior numbers to those of his opponents, so that his name was feared throughout the land.

She realised at once that somehow she must assist him to escape – she a defenceless woman against these uncouth soldiers who were demanding food and drink, good bedding for themselves and fodder for their horses. They led their prisoner into the Guard Room, but Agnes pleaded that she be allowed to take him up to her room to attend to a sword-thrust which had penetrated his right arm. Leaving him on her couch to steep his wound in warm water, she hastened below to organise a meal for Montrose's escort with a brew of strong ale that she felt sure would induce deep sleep.

She then warned one of her trusty retainers to have a horse saddled and waiting, and that when someone came in the darkness and said 'Ceud mille failte', meaning 'A hundred thousand welcomes' in the Gaelic, that he was to be allowed to ride the horse away.

It was two o'clock and the moon was rising, when going along to Montrose's room she gently woke him, and pulling back an arras on the wall showed him a shaft that led down to a secret tunnel by which he could crawl away unseen from the castle. She bade him go quickly and told him how to find the waiting horse, and also the passwords that he was to give to the groom waiting with the horse. He paused beside the shaft and embraced this brave kinswoman of his, but knowing well what fate would befall her, and probably her husband, too, when he returned, he refused to go, saying to her, 'Sooner than go down that hole I will meet my accusers in Edinburgh.' The dawn came and the cavalcade departed, taking their prisoner still riding the decrepit pony which had already brought him all the way from Ardvreck Castle in Sutherland.

Ten days passed and Lady Leslie, on going into the room that

Montrose had slept in, found a robin perched on the bed. She asked the little bird how it had managed to get into the house, and then she remembered what the 'Guid wifee of Glack' had said to her in rhyme. Catching the little messenger with her hands, she released it from a window. Somehow she knew that this was a warning of news to come that her dear Jamie Graham, Marquis, Statesman and General, had been taken to the scaffold in Edinburgh where he had gone to meet his accusers, and his arch-enemy the Duke of Argyll, who a few years later was to meet the same fate.

A month passed and Sir John Leslie had returned home, so he was able to receive and give hospitality to young Prince Charles (later King Charles II) who arrived at Pitcaple having landed from exile at Garmouth at the mouth of the River Spey. A banquet was hastily prepared and John Leslie was persuaded to join the Prince's retinue and growing army which subsequently invaded England. Then again a robin appeared within the castle, the forerunner of the bitter news that the Laird had been killed at the Battle of Worcester, where the Prince avoided capture by hiding in an oak tree and thus escaping to Holland, from whence he returned ten years later to be made King.

It is still the same at Pitcaple today with the robins appearing inside the house to warn that sad news is coming, and you can see that shaft which could have helped Montrose to escape, and the room he slept in that night in 1650. (The last time a robin appeared was in December 1978; shortly afterwards news came that a cousin, of whom the writer was very fond, had recently died.)

The Maiden Stone

Pitcaple lies at the foot of the Grampian hill range that is called 'Bennachie', and at its eastern end it rises to a steep point culminating in a small platform of rock. This is surrounded by a fairly massive fortification of stonework that may have been formed during the era of the Picts, who at one time ruled this part of Scotland. This feature is known as 'Mither Tap' (Mither in Aberdeenshire being Mother), and the outline of Bennachie viewed from afar is not unlike a woman's breast, indeed it is said that the word Bennachie means just that. High up on the northern side of

113

Bennachie is a round mound that is marked on the Ordnance Map 'Maiden Castle', which is easily identifiable and on which there must have been a motte or wooden castle, although this building has long since disappeared. Not far away from the Maiden Castle beside the public road running from Chapel of Garioch to the present-day Bennachie Car Park, there stands a monolith or single upright stone, which is called 'The Maiden Stone', and the question is often asked as to why it is so named.

The legend or story is that there lived near by a beautiful girl called Janet of Drumdurno. One day Janet was baking some bread and while it was in the oven she took up her hand-mirror to comb her lovely long hair which hung down to her waist. Suddenly in the mirror she saw that there was a dark man with a black cloak standing behind her, so she turned and confronted this stranger. He announced that he had come to seek her hand in marriage having always admired her beauty, and indeed was prepared to arrange for the wedding to take place the very next day.

Janet was somewhat overcome and naturally refused this sudden offer, so the stranger then said that if he could build a 'causeway' from Drumdurno right up to Mither Tap before midnight, would she agree to marry him? As this condition seemed utterly impossible for the stranger to accomplish, Janet agreed, hoping to be rid of this man.

There was a full moon that night and so just before midnight Janet looked up towards Mither Tap to see how far the stranger had succeeded in building his causeway, and to her utter horror she saw that there was a causeway, or as it is called in the Gaelic a 'maden', leading right up the hill.

Janet was filled with fear, especially when she thought she saw the stranger approaching, so she fled from her dwelling hoping to hide from this man whom she did not want to marry in spite of her promise.

Before she had gone far through the night she became frozen with fear and rooted to the ground like a pillar of stone, which may have been a spell cast upon her by this warlock who was the Devil himself.

ƆUNROBIN CASTLE

Dunrobin Castle, the historic seat of the Earls and Dukes of Sutherland, is situated on a natural platform overlooking the Moray Firth, near Golspie. This once provided a good vantage point, and now acts as a stage to display the castle's splendours. Originally, a massive inner keep was built about 1275 and the main structure was erected a century later. The next addition – a large fortified mansion with a central courtyard – was made in the seventeenth century. Most of the basic structure remains in its original form, but more additions in the nineteenth century further altered its outward appearance.

Spanning as it does many centuries, Dunrobin Castle has born witness to numerous changes. In the early nineteenth century it saw the misery caused by the Clearances, the Golspie district being central in the disputes between evicted tenants and their landlords. During the First World War it became a naval hospital, and between 1963 and 1972 it was used as a boys' public school. All the while, it has remained a Sutherland possession, and it acts as a living monument to Scottish history.

The story which follows was written by Miss Clare Banks.

Opening times:
Early April, Easter weekend, May – mid October
Daily 10.30–17.30*, except Sun 13.00–17.30*
(*closes 1 hour earlier in April, May and October)
Other dates by appointment
Tel: (01408) 633177; Fax: (01408) 633800

Over 200 years before the Victorian innovations and additions to Dunrobin Castle, the building had a very different character. There were no fairy-tale spires adorning the roof, no imposing staterooms, no sign of the luxurious opulence of the nineteenth century. In those days, the castle stood as a rugged stronghold, a much smaller and altogether simpler edifice, whose main purpose was to protect the Earl and his family from unwelcome marauders, not merely to serve as a civilised Highland retreat.

Parts of the original building are over 700 years old so it is fair to say there must be many a mournful and unhappy being still walking its stone-flagged floors. But the most tragic of them all must surely be Margaret, daughter of the fourteenth Earl, who lost her life in a desperate attempt to elope with the man she loved, the man her father had forbidden her ever to see again.

It is said that this beautiful but ill-fated maiden still wanders the dusty passages of the older part of the castle (to be seen looking across the inner courtyard from the Queen's Corridor). Often her sobs, bewailing her father's injustice towards her and the loss of her life and her love, can be heard echoing dismally from one small room – a strange, dark chamber, lit by a single, narrow window, which has a very apparent, almost oppressive atmosphere of great unhappiness.

Margaret's story is a common one, even by today's standards. She fell deeply in love with one Jamie Gunn, the younger son of one of the Earl's tacksmen. A brave, handsome lad but one with few prospects and vain hope of claiming a Chief's daughter as his wife.

However, as the violent storms and chill blasts of the Highland winter gave way to the soft sunshine and gentle showers of the northern spring, Fortune smiled on the two lovers for a few brief weeks. Their love for one another strengthened with each day that dawned. Every moment was precious to them; each tender kiss worth a thousand times more than all the Earl's worldly riches; and, as a lasting reminder of the love they shared, Jamie carved their entwined initials on a weathered rock that still stands at the entrance to a cave on the hillside of Dunrobin Glen.

The two lovers attempted to keep their regard for one another secret, both knowing that the Earl, in his position as Chief of the Clan

Sutherland, would have no choice or inclination but to disapprove of their match. But alas, love can often lead to rashness and an ill-timed meeting between the young couple revealed the true situation.

Once their secret was out, Jamie took his courage in both hands and approached the Earl to ask his permission to wed his fair daughter. What passed between the two of them, history does not relate, but the outcome dashed all hopes for the luckless pair. The Earl, by repute a quick-tempered man, appeared outraged at Jamie's impudence and dismissed him as an 'impoverished rapscallion', not fit to kiss the ground his daughter walked upon. Such was his rage, that he forbad young Jamie ever to darken the doors of Dunrobin again.

Margaret, utterly distraught at this turn of events, pleaded, begged and implored her father to change his mind. He stood firm, so finally, as a last resort, she attempted to run away but was thwarted by the Earl's Steward who had been assigned to keep a watchful eye on her in the likelihood of just such an occurrence.

This, together with her spirited and adamant refusal to receive the man her father deemed suitable as her husband, led the Earl to take the drastic step of imprisoning her in the dark attic room, with its single window overlooking the castle surrounds. The room could only be reached by way of the keep stairs and the Earl placed a guard at the bottom of the steps to prevent any further attempts at escape.

For hours on end, Margaret would stand by the narrow casement of her gloomy chamber, gazing up towards the cave on the hillside – scene of so many blissful encounters. The sweet memories of those happier times tormented her day and night; but her trust in Jamie never faltered, somehow he would find a way of rescuing her. Each day, her belief in her lover enabled her to face her father with an undaunted spirit that was adamant in its refusal to bow down to his cruel demands. But when darkness fell, and she was left alone in her misery, Margaret's anguish could no longer be contained. On still nights, the muffled sound of her impassioned sobs reached to every corner of the castle, touching every soul who heard them – except for the iron-hearted Earl himself.

Margaret's only saviour in the depths of her despair was her maid, Morag, who still attended her. Morag, a simple Highland lass, watching her mistress grow pale and wasted as the days wore on, was deeply moved by such obvious distress. Margaret was dying of a broken heart. Bravely, the little maid offered to liaise between Margaret and Jamie, hoping that she could help them find some means of escape.

Morag got word to the ever-faithful Jamie, safely lodged with sympathetic kinsfolk in the Strath of Kildonan, and together they devised a plan to rescue the fair Margaret. Morag was to hide a length of rope beneath her kirtle and smuggle it up to the attic room when she took up Margaret's supper. For his part, Jamie was to have two horses waiting in the castle grounds, safely concealed from prying eyes, and would arrange for a boat to be hove to at Little Ferry, ready to take him and his love down the coast to Edinburgh, far away from the wilds of Sutherland.

On the night in question, Morag dutifully delivered the rope to Margaret's room and tried to calm her mistress who was almost beside herself with nerves and the prospect of seeing her beloved once more.

At the given signal, a stone thrown up to the narrow window, Margaret let the free end of the rope run out over the stone sill, Morag having previously secured the other end to a stout oak settle.

'My love!' Margaret called down softly. 'Is it truly you?'

'Aye, I'm here, dearest!' came Jamie's eager reply. 'But make haste, my sweeting, we have not a moment to spare!'

But that moment had passed already. The Earl's Steward, a cunning sycophant, tainted with guile, had learnt at the very last hour of what was afoot. His devious mind had reckoned on just such an attempt being made and he had been careful to post another such evil being as himself to keep a close yet clandestine eye on Jamie's whereabouts.

So it was that at the critical moment, just as Margaret had mounted the ledge and was about to lower herself down the rope, the door of her dark and dismal chamber burst open to reveal her father, the Earl himself! 'Stop! Go no further!' he roared, as he hurled himself across the room. 'Never will you marry that rascal!'

Shocked by the sound of her father's angry voice and already weakened by her long, miserable days of imprisonment, Margaret's grip faltered. Numbed by terror, she slipped and, with a last despairing cry of, 'Then I shall marry nobody!', she fell to the ground and to her death.

Jamie, seeing his love fall, immediately ran to her lifeless form and cradled her in his arms for a single instant. But even in the terrible agony of his grief, he realised he had no time to spare if he was not to meet the same horrible fate.

With one last, despairing look at the pale face of the girl he'd loved so dearly, he mounted his horse and addressed the Earl who, shocked beyond measure, was still standing at the window above. 'May she haunt you for ever more!' Jamie's passionate tones rang out. Then he spurred his steed and disappeared into the dark night, alone and forever banished from his beloved and their homeland.

Footnote

There are still people, even among those who work at Dunrobin, who express a certain degree of scepticism regarding the existence of Margaret's mournful spirit. Nevertheless, not long ago, we were provided with what would appear to be unequivocal proof of her presence. One of the castle employees was sent up to the haunted floor in order to bring down some china which was stored in an attic there. She knew nothing of the ghost story but, being a gregarious type, took her dog along with her for company. Just before they reached the door of the room which had held Margaret captive for so long, the dog whined, dug his claws into the wooden floor-boards of the passage, and refused to move.

fasque

Fasque lies in the parish of Fettercairn to the west of Laurencekirk, about fifteen miles north of Montrose. Sir Alexander Ramsay began building the present house in 1809, the architect being possibly John Paterson of Edinburgh. Sir Alexander's son, also named Alexander and who succeeded his father a year later, continued the work over the next three or four years. The estate was sold in 1829 to John Gladstone, father of the Prime Minister, William Gladstone.

The house is Classical in style, although castellated. The interior has much fine plasterwork and Classical detailing. The domestic quarters retain most of their original furnishings and equipment, including a splendid collection of copper kettles, jelly-moulds, saucepans and other implements in the kitchen.

Fasque is now the home of Mr and Mrs Peter Gladstone. The article which follows was written by Mr Peter Gladstone.

Opening times:
May–September
Daily 13.30–17.30, except Fri; evenings for groups by appointment
Tel: (01561) 340202; Fax: (01561) 340325

The Spirits of Fasque

Fasque is the most haunted house I know. Though a delightfully happy place, it seems to have three generations of the last century around in broad daylight – or perhaps they have just gone out for a walk. No 'ghost' has been seen, but spirits abound in every room. Their moods depend upon your mood – and the weather. They may at times be stern, but they are never unkind.

We enter the main back entrance under the carriage archway and young John Lough, the boy (in 1900) slips back into the Boots-and-Knives Hall. We have no firm evidence that he was making shy approaches to Emma, the under dairymaid (of 1876). She will be turning the handle of the butter table in the next-door room to extract the surplus water after her hard morning on the paddle churn. Is it Dingle the Head Gamekeeper, or Hanslip the Keeper from the Lake Cottage, who stands aside to let us pass through the back door? It was surely one of them, for hanging in the meat and game larder are a hare and some grouse. Mary, the fifteen-year-old kitchen maid, changes her headlong dash down the stairs from the girl servants' quarters to a more deferential pace. Doubtless she was sent up to adjust her hair and cap, an operation she had twice been distinctly told was not acceptable in the kitchen.

The kitchen strikes us as a mass of copper. Mrs Kee, the Housekeeper, simply notices (1899) that it is rather hot with the huge open fire, and takes Mr Knight, the head of ten gardeners, into the vegetable scullery to discuss the day's needs. Diminutive Jemina Towns, the scullery maid aged thirteen, is skinning rabbits for broth in the main scullery beyond. Thick broth, of a different variety each day, was made in the Fasque kitchens and carried, together with fresh hot bread, to the estate school a quarter of a mile away. This provided a very welcome, far more solid than liquid, midday meal. Miss Towns lived all her days at The Old Mains near the school. The daughter of the estate wheelwright, she started work at thirteen, rising at five-thirty each morning to scrub the kitchen table. At six Mary came to sweep up the sawdust on the floor, and then between them they scrubbed a quarter of the floor each morning, put down fresh sawdust for the grease drips and were out by the time that breakfast cooking started at seven. In later years she looked after my generation as children, and then at well over eighty she was the regular friend and baby-sitter of my children. She died peacefully at the age of eighty-five and was sadly missed by all. It is from her that many of the rituals and ways of doing things have been handed down, so we now know what is really authentic.

Next door to the kitchen, bread was prepared for the bakery by the still-room maids, who also boiled the morning eggs and made the coffee. We feel (the ignorant might say 'imagine') McBean, the left-handed butler, as he comes out of the butler's pantry in his green baize apron. A house party is obviously staying and he has to lend a hand with the cleaning of the silver, which is proving too much for the two busy footmen. He is not, today, just the overlord. . . . The candle table is set out by McBean himself. The Laird and his wife's candles are the big brass ones on the right-hand end, ready to go upstairs when called for. A couple of rows along from these are the nursery candles in their red double 'safety' holders. At the far left-hand end are the plain holders with the candles for the lower servants. But all are put down left handed. If you do not think a candle-holder can be put down left handed, try picking one up from the middle with your right hand. The family expression of 'doing a McBean' still means 'putting something the wrong way round'.

We have passed through the dining-room, across the hall, and gone up the superb double cantilevered staircase. We arrive in Sir Thomas's bedroom assured that this will be no intrusion, but he has surely just left it for a stroll (1870?), for some second sense tells us he is not far off. Being a room without the spirits present, we can snoop a little further. The height of the mattresses on the four-poster shows us the need for the bed steps. The housemaid must have heard us coming and slipped out, for the little cupboard that makes the top step is ajar showing the decorated domestic article which in some more vulgar households might be found beneath the bed.

Will it be all right to peep through the door opposite or will the family and their guests be seated there? We enter the drawing-room, a long south-facing room on the first floor flooded with light from the large windows. Miss Mary as an old lady, or perhaps as a ten-year-old girl, has just left. It doesn't matter what age she is at today. She spent her whole life here after her grandfather's death and her father's inheritance and nothing was changed or needing change during it. Everything was quite good enough and there was no need to throw anything out. Today we sense her as an elderly lady of considerable height, very generous yet at the same time frugal. But there is surely someone in the library beyond, through the double maghogany doors. Young William, aged twenty-three, is discussing the new classical volumes he has brought his father back from London with the elderly gentleman whose portrait we surely saw in the dining-room. William Ewart Gladstone was not only four times Prime Minister, but also presented thirteen Budgets as Chancellor of the Exchequer. His father John emigrated from his native Scotland to Liverpool to seek his fortune as a lad. He returned and bought Fasque from Sir Alexander Ramsay in 1829 having made his fortune and reared a large family.

Who else is around? We know so many of their names and so much about them. The two daughters of Hanslip the Keeper are weeding in the garden. Elsie, the older of the two, has the big barrow filled with weeds and cuttings, and Laura Thomson is wheeling away another. Mrs Horton, the Verger of the Episcopalian chapel near the car park; Maggie Thow the head laundry-maid; Mr Clark the cattleman; Mr Cullus the head coachman, and later when the first car came the 'mechanician'; young John Smith who later became head gardener; Allison who broke the Clydesdales; Miss Helen (William and Thomas's sister) dressed in dreary black: all these people are here in spirit.

How have all these spirits stayed at Fasque? Some say it is because the house and contents are so complete, and yet the place is in no way a museum with items collected from other establishments. It is not a collection – it is just Fasque. John the first bought it in 1829. His eldest son Tom inherited when his family was young, and that was, in 100 years, the family of children that lived here. Their toys are still out. Of the family, Bobby, the second Sir John, and his sister Mary lived here as bachelor and spinster until their deaths in 1926 and 1932 respectively. At the peak there were twenty-six indoor servants. Now we trip over the Wellington boots of the first Sir John's great-great-great-grandchildren (which perhaps should have been put away before our visit but are still lying in the middle of the floor in the Gun Room). I would say it is an insensitive person and not just an unimaginative one who does not meet the spirits at Fasque. Of course a conducted tour would spoil that – but with our own time to walk round there is time to meet and sense them all. I hope we never have to have organised 'conducted tours'. On your visit you will not have time to 'meet' all those who are still with us in spirit, but you will surely meet some.

mellerstain

The superb Georgian mansion of Mellerstain stands south of Gordon on the road to Kelso. The house was begun in 1725 to a design by William Adam, who built the east and west wings. They were to have been joined by a Dutch Palladian-style centre-piece, but this was never built. It was left to William's son Robert to design, in 1770, the magnificent central block we see today. Many of the rooms have beautiful Adam decorative schemes and are in their original colours. Mellerstain is rare among great houses in retaining a domestic rather than stately atmosphere, being spacious but not overwhelming in scale, and full of charm.

Mellerstain is the home of Lord Binning, son and heir of the Earl of Haddington.

The Mellerstain Trust

Opening times:
May, June and September
Wed, Fri and Sun 12.30–17.00
July–August
Daily 12.30–17.00, except Sat
Tel: (01573) 410225

Mellerstain has been the home of the Baillie family for 350 years, having been granted by Royal Charter to George Baillie of Jerviswood in 1642. His son, Robert, inherited the estate in 1646. In 1676 he was imprisoned in the Edinburgh Tolbooth and fined £500, as a punishment for rescuing his brother-in-law from what he believed to have been an illegal arrest. He was later arrested once more, this time for High Treason, since he was a Covenanter. The future Earl of Marchmont, then Sir Patrick Hume, wanted to send a message to Robert while he was imprisoned. If the attempt had been discovered, it would have exposed Sir Patrick in turn to possible retribution by the authorities. Therefore, instead of taking the message himself, he decided to send his daughter, Grisell, then only twelve years old. It is clear that even at this age Grisell had already shown her strength of character, since it is unlikely that the task would have been entrusted to a child unless she was considered exceptionally reliable and brave. Grisell carried out the difficult task successfully, but soon had further opportunities to show her trustworthiness.

Robert Baillie was finally executed, and due to the political and religious climate Sir Patrick considered it safer to go into hiding. The hiding-place he chose was in the vaults of Polwarth Church, a mile from his home. For a long, nerve-racking month he had only Grisell to rely on for daily food and drink, and she never failed him. Then the situation became too dangerous, and Sir Patrick, his estates forfeit, decided to flee to the Low Countries.

He stayed in exile for three and a half years, his family sharing the misery of a hand-to-mouth existence. Also living in Holland at this time was George Baillie, Robert's son, who with his father's estates forfeit led an equally impecunious existence. George and Grisell gradually came to know each other, but it was not until 1692 that they were married, after William of Orange had been invited to take over the throne of England. Sir Patrick and George sailed to England in the Prince's train, and regained their forfeited estates.

As châtelaine of Mellerstain, Grisell was outstanding, both as housewife and mother. From 1693 onwards, she kept a Household Book in which she maintained meticulous records of every item of income and expenditure at Mellerstain. She also noted down Rules for Staff, recipes, housekeeping hints, medicinal cures and details of foreign travel: everything, in fact, which could possibly be said to relate to the running of a large country house in the eighteenth century. All the entries were written in longhand by Lady Grisell herself; she would surely have been glad to know that her books are preserved today at Mellerstain, to delight and inform us two centuries later. To give some flavour of the variety and attention to detail in the books, some extracts follow:

From the book of Medicinal Cures:

For a Foul Face

Pour some brandy on flower of Brimstone, shake it every day it will settle to the bottom, at night wash your face with the brandy, it will make it come out very thick all over, therefor for a week that you use it, keep within doors and catch not cold.

Sore throat

Persley beat in a mortar, mixt with the white of raw egg, beat up to a pultice and aplyd to the throat.

From a Recipe Book:

Baked Bread Pudding

Pour a pint of boiling milk upon as much sliced bread as will soak up all the milk, cover it up close and when it is almost cold stir into it 3 eggs leaving out one of the whites, a quarter of a pound of sugar, a little grated nutmeg, a very little salt, then put it in a little china bason or a dish and bake it.

Details of Foreign Travel:

Frankfort to Collogne

We went by water doun the Rhine in two days and a half. We hierd two boats, one for ourselves close coverd like a Pleasur Barge upon the Tames, in which we lay all night upon good straw and Pillows for our heads. An open boat for the servants and chaises. We payd 75 Florins for all, Taxes included, of which there are many at every toun you pass by. It was in the sumer and no danger of catching cold. We caryd our provitions had tea water boyld and every thing dresst in the boat with the servants which was tyd to ours. The water men or servants went on shore at any toun we came to and got us what ever we wanted.

kelBURN castle

Kelburn Castle stands just south of the town of Largs, looking out over the Firth of Clyde and the islands of Cumbrae, Bute and Arran with the Mull of Kintyre in the background. The Boyle family, created Earls of Glasgow in 1703, have owned Kelburn since the twelfth century and the Old Keep, which forms part of the present castle, is thought to date from this period. Although the castle is not open to the public on a day-to-day basis, interested visitors who make a written application will be shown round this fascinating home, with its mixture of styles which give great individuality to the different rooms.

The Kelburn Country Centre, established on the estate in 1977 with the aid of a grant from the Countryside Commission for Scotland, provides many outdoor recreational activities in the beautiful setting of the Kelburn Glen, where winding paths lead to spectacular waterfalls and magnificent views.

The delightful walled garden contains rare shrubs and trees, and the Water Garden, set beside a series of little burns, contains a bamboo jungle as bewildering as any maze.

The story which follows was written by Rear Admiral The Earl of Glasgow.

Kelburn Country Centre

Opening times:
Kelburn Country Centre (Secret Forest)
Easter – mid October
Daily 09.00–18.00
Tel: (01475) 568685; Fax: (01475) 568121
Kelburn Castle
July–August
14.00–16.00 (guided tours only)

The Boyles of Kelburn

There seems little doubt that the family of De Boyville (later to become Boyle) came to England with William the Conqueror in 1066. They were a large family and settled in various parts of the country, in Wales and in Cumberland. The Welsh branch went later to Ireland and were the ancestors of the Earls of Cork and Shannon.

When David I came to the throne of Scotland in 1124, having spent all his early life at the Norman Court in London, he invited a number of his Norman friends to accompany him. Among these was a powerful Baron called Hugh de Moreville, whom David appointed Hereditary Great Constable of Scotland and gave him, with other lands, the Baronies of Cunningham and Largs which included most of North Ayrshire. My branch of the de Boyvilles were related to the de Morevilles by marriage and came to Scotland with him. When de Moreville divided up his lands among his friends and relations under the old feudal system, the de Boyvilles were given the Lands of Kelburn, which did not then include the Barony of Fairlie. Though documentary evidence is lacking, it seems fairly certain that the de Boyvilles got their lands of Kelburn from Hugh de Moreville about 1140.

The experts tell me that the first thing a family did when it received its land was to build itself a motte to establish ownership and to make its mark with the local inhabitants.

A motte, as I understand it, was a cluster of wooden huts with wooden defensive walls surrounding it. Various professors who have visited Kelburn all agree that our motte must have been on the site of the present castle. It was a good defensive position.

The experts are hopelessly divided as to the date at which families started building in stone. Their assessments vary between 1200 and 1400. One knows of castles in Scotland reputed to have been built before 1200, without counting churches and abbeys. Being a Norman family, accustomed to stone castles in Normandy and England, it is my contention that the Old Keep of Kelburn was started about 1200. Alas, there are no written records.

The Old Keep consisted of a solid square tower with a round tower and a turret at the north-east and south-east corners respectively. At the north-west corner was the round tower containing the old stone stairs, which climb from the first floor to the top. This tower still sticks out from the side of the 1580 castle and was probably corbelled at the first-floor level rather like the old turret.

On the ground floor is the old front door which now opens on to the kitchen passage of the Victorian wing. It has large heavy hinges which must have carried the oak door and the wall at this level is four and a half feet thick.

The roof was almost certainly flat. We do not know whether it was battlemented or whether it had a small stone structure in the middle as is the case in some old Scots castles.

We held our land from the de Morevilles until 1196 when the male line died out and passed through a daughter to Roland, Lord of Galloway. In 1234 the male line of the Lords of Galloway failed and the lands passed to a daughter, Dervogilla, who married John de Balliol. Their son, John Balliol, succeeded to the throne of Scotland in 1292 and from that date onwards we have held our lands from the Crown.

The family (by now called Boyle) fought under Alexander III at the Battle of Largs in 1263 and under Walter the Steward at the Battle of Bannockburn in 1314. The eldest son of the Laird was killed fighting for James III at the Battle of Sauchieburn in 1488 and another elder son was killed at the Battle of Pinkie in 1547.

In 1568 John Boyle of Kelburn raised 100 men and marched them over the hill to fight for Mary Queen of Scots. On his way he received news of her defeat at the Battle of Langside and her flight to England and turned sadly home. It was this Laird who, in 1580, decided to build on to the Old Keep. He increased the size of the building by two more barrel roofs on the ground floor. He built the 1580 stair tower on the south-west corner to balance the old tower and a turret on the north-west corner to balance the old turret. The style of his new tower and turret appear to have been exactly copied from the old ones. He then roofed the old and his new bit as one with a steep slate roof, so from the outside it is not immediately obvious that the eastern end is much older than 1580.

He built his front door on the south side of the house and his initials and those of his wife are carved in stone above it and, higher up, the arms of Boyle of Kelburn and the date 1581. Most of the principal bedrooms are now contained in the 1580 castle with larder and cellar on the ground floor. We still occupy the Old Keep. (*Most of what is written about this part of the castle in* Castellated and Domestic Architecture in Scotland, *Volume 4, by Macgibbon and Ross, is incorrect. As this work is regarded by many as the Bible of Old Scottish Castles, it is frequently quoted and reproduced to our intense irritation. If a date could be established for the building of the Old Keep, we would have a strong claim to be the oldest castle in Scotland, inhabited by the same family.*)

John Boyle's son died leaving no male heir and Kelburn passed to his daughter Grizel who married her cousin, David Boyle of Halkshill. This David was a great-grandson of John Boyle of Ballikewin, second son of John Boyle of Kelburn, and his father had acquired the lands of Halkshill in 1617 and made a small fortune out of shipping. In 1657 David Boyle (now of Kelburn) acquired the Barony of Fairlie which has remained with the family to this day.

It was Grizel's grandson, David Boyle of Kelburn (1666–1733), who became a distinguished Scottish statesman, a Privy Councillor and Lord of the Treasury among other appointments – and was created Lord Boyle in 1699 and Viscount of Kelburn and Earl of Glasgow, all in the Peerage of Scotland, in 1703. He was a strong supporter and personal friend of the second Duke of Queensberry and played an important part in getting the Act of Union of 1707 through the Scottish Parliament. For reasons unknown he sold Halkshill in 1694. It was he who ordered the construction of the Mansion House, joined to the old castle at its south-eastern end and completed in 1700. This is a fine example of a Scottish mansion of the time of William and Mary, and was built by Thomas Caldwell. There is little doubt that the Laird himself played a big part in the design and layout both inside and out. The Mansion House is attached to the old castle at an angle on its north side. With its crow-foot gables, walled forecourt and 'plaisaunce' garden the feeling is French rather than English or Scots.

On either side of the front door on the north side are the original lead drainpipes and, above the door, a rather splendid double-headed eagle, also in lead, which the Earl took as his crest. Higher up, carved in stone, are the initials of the first Earl and his two wives.

The front door leads into a hall and from thence up a high stair-well to the first floor. On the right a door leads into the drawing-room. This is a lovely room by any standards; a double cube running the whole width of the house from north to south. It has retained its original 1700 cornice and cove and the panelled walls, doors, window frames and shutters are decorated in gold-leaf on cream with a background of pale blue. We are fairly certain that the decoration and colour scheme were executed by the third Earl in the second half of the eighteenth century. When we had to do up this room in 1966 we could not improve on the original and so reproduced it as it had been.

This part of the house also contains two bedrooms, a library, sitting-rooms and a gun-room area.

John, the second Earl (1688–1740), from whom my branch of the family is descended, only survived his father by seven years.

John, the third Earl (1714–75) and his wife, The Honourable Elizabeth Ross, a considerable heiress, clearly loved Kelburn and did much for the house and grounds. He joined the army in 1744 and a most moving monument to him in the Kelburn Glen records that at the Battle of Fontenoy, early in life, he lost his hand and his health and at the Battle of Lafteld he received two wounds in one attack. He was Lord High Commissioner to the General Assembly of the Church of Scotland from 1764 to 1772.

George, the fourth Earl (1765–1843), was a very considerable landowner with estates in Ayrshire, Cumbrae, Renfrewshire, Fife and Northumberland. After an early army career he became Lord-Lieutenant of Renfrewshire in 1810 and of Ayrshire in 1820, Lord Rector of Glasgow University in 1817 and was a Representative Peer of Scotland from 1790 to 1815. In 1815 he was created a Baron of the United Kingdom with the title of Baron Ross of Hawkshead. This was a revival of the extinct title of his mother's family which died out again with the death of his fourth son, the sixth Earl of Glasgow.

His eldest son, Lord Boyle, served in the Royal Navy during the Napoleonic Wars and was captured at sea after a gallant resistance and imprisoned at Verdun from 1807 to 1814. He died unmarried in 1818 and his brother succeeded to the title.

James, the fifth Earl (1792–1869) was styled Viscount Kelburn after the death of his brother. This formidable and eccentric character also served in the Royal Navy but in 1839 was elected Member of Parliament for Ayrshire and held his seat until he succeeded to the title. He was Lord-Lieutenant of Renfrewshire from 1844. He was Master of the Lanark and Renfrew Hunt for many years and was one of the great figures of the English turf in the middle of the last century as a breeder and owner of racehorses. He was a member of the Jockey Club for thirty years and, though he won the Two Thousand Guineas shortly before his death, the Derby and the St Leger always eluded him. In about 1850 he built the wall round the Kelburn Policies, which still stands to this day, to give employment to the local people who had fallen on hard times. He died without children.

George Frederick, the sixth Earl (1825–90), succeeded his half-brother who was thirty-three years his senior. At Oxford, early in life, he got swept up with the religious controversies of the day, the Pre-Raphaelites and the Gothic Revival and, at the age of twenty-five, commissioned the architect Butterfield to build him a Cathedral and Theological College on the Island of Cumbrae. He continued to build and endow churches all over Scotland until about the middle of the 1880s, when it became clear that the money was running out. All the very extensive family lands were put up to auction and he was only saved from the bankruptcy court by my grandfather, his cousin and heir, who sold his Estate of Shewalton (near Irvine), bought back Kelburn and put virtually all the money, which was secured on him as heir to the title, towards paying off the debts for the honour of the family. George Frederick is much revered in many parts of Scotland, including Cumbrae, but is not popular with the family. It was he, however, who built the Victorian wing in 1879–80; the beauty of so many old Scots houses was ruined by such a wing, but ours is not offensive and is in many ways a considerable asset.

The main block is built out from the north-east corner of the 1700 Mansion House to the north and east. Its principal windows face out to the west across the forecourt to the Firth of Clyde. It then wraps itself round the Old Keep on two sides with a wide uneven stone passage between on the ground floor.

On this floor is a spacious Victorian kitchen; on the first floor are the dining-room and nurseries. The dining-room is of some interest. The wallpaper, curtains and door furniture are all original William Morris. Above the dining-room is a billiard room and two bachelor bedrooms.

After the sixth Earl of Glasgow had gone virtually bankrupt in 1888 and my grandfather, his second cousin, had surrendered what was left of his inheritance to keep him out of the bankruptcy court, the family were fairly hard up. My grandfather succeeded as seventh Earl in 1890 and had moved into Kelburn a year earlier with his family.

He accepted the appointment of Governor of New Zealand in 1893 partly in the hope of being able to live on his salary and expenses and save some of his own money. The hope was not fulfilled and he returned to Kelburn five years later £1500 worse off. On leaving New Zealand he was created a peer of the United Kingdom with the title of Baron Fairlie of Fairlie.

On his return to Kelburn in 1897, my grandfather, despite his poverty, seems to have lived in considerable style. He employed a number of servants in the house and a considerable number of estate workers, shepherds and foresters. The Home Farm, a cluster of attractive old buildings across the Glen from the castle and always known as the 'South Offices', was in full swing. There were carthorses in the stable, cows in the byre, pigs in the pigsties and hens in the henhouse. There was a dairy and a laundry staffed with girls who lived in the bothies. Peacocks roamed wild in the woods and used to come over with the pheasants. They were in great danger of being shot despite cries of 'Ware peacock!'

My grandmother was a Hunter Blair and a very attractive person. She was a formidable hostess and a relentless matchmaker. She kept the house constantly filled with guests and with a large and high-spirited family, who had to sleep in the attics to make room for the visitors, Kelburn must have been a riot.

Despite the cheapness of labour in those days, my grandmother's extravagance undoubtedly told on my grandfather and after the turn of the century there are gaps in the Visitors' Book when Kelburn had to be let and the family retired to a Victorian villa in Ardrossan to recoup.

My grandfather died in 1915 and by the end of the First World War the glory had to some extent departed. The Home Farm had been given up, though there were still two carthorses working and one last magnificent peacock which stalked round the South Offices. The buildings, except those inhabited by estate workers, degenerated into storehouses for animal feeds and repositories for old furniture but both my father and I went to considerable lengths to keep them wind- and watertight.

During the fifty years which followed my grandfather's death, the problem which faced my father, and later myself, was that the estate could never really cover the maintenance of the house and garden. After three generations of naval officers the family finances had not improved and, as taxes increased and wages soared, life became very difficult. Twice in the 1920s, my father let Kelburn for considerable periods and he, my mother and the family (there were five of us) retired to small villas in inexpensive parts of France. This was the greatest fun for us children but worrying for my parents.

My father tried various things – rabbit warrens, letting the shooting, building a teahouse on the most perfect site, known as the 'Bonnie Blink' and taking in paying guests. The teahouse was a great success as long as my sisters were the waitresses but rather lost its glamour and popularity when they gave up. In the 1920s my father sold six farms and I subsequently leased the Kelburn Park to the local golf club and sold off a few fields in the village of Fairlie for development. My father made over the estate to me in 1946 and lived on at Kelburn until he died at the age of eighty-nine in 1963. I retired from the Navy the same year.

Between 1963 and 1969 my wife and I, with some help from Historic Buildings, did up the house from top to bottom. It was a mammoth task but very rewarding. In 1973 I made over the estate to my son Patrick, Viscount Kelburn, but my wife and I retained the house and garden. In 1975 my son and his wife came up to Scotland and he took a real grip on the estate and started turning the South Offices into the Kelburn Country Centre. The stable became a café. The cow byre a weaver's workshop, the laundry a shop. One of the old cottages became a tack-room to support pony-trekking and there was an exhibition room. He constructed an adventure course, a children's playground and pets' corner. In 1977 the estate was opened to the public and we allowed most of the gardens to be visited, too. My son resurrected old paths in the very beautiful Kelburn Glen, repaired others and constructed new bridges over the burn.

The venture was an immediate success. There is nothing comparable in North Ayrshire or Renfrewshire and the site is ideal for views across the Firth to the islands, dominated by the peaks of Arran.

This gallant attempt to restore the family fortunes, involving very hard work, is at the moment thwarted by the excessively high bank rate. It was not cheap to set up; nevertheless we all have hopes for the future.

In many old family homes in Scotland a similar saga could be recorded. If it is considered to be in the national interest that old houses and castles of great beauty should continue to be inhabited by families who have owned and loved them for centuries, some financial help is required. Much has already been done but the costs of repair and maintenance are now so astronomic that even with some assistance it is difficult for families to make up the difference.

CRAIGIEVAR CASTLE

Craigievar Castle is a fairy-tale castle in the front rank of European architecture. Set in the secluded hilly country of Aberdeenshire, it is on the A980, six miles south of Alford and some twenty-six miles from Aberdeen. The castle was bought from the Forbes-Sempill family by a consortium of benefactors and presented to the National Trust for Scotland in 1963.

Stewart Cruden in his book The Scottish Castle *states that 'Craigievar Castle ranks with any representative building in Britain'. Completed in 1626 for a colourful Forbes Laird known as Danzig Willie, the superb building has never been marred by any additions. To quote Stewart Cruden again: 'It has a serene assurance not communicated by any other tower house however pleasing.'*

The simplicity of its lower walls, which rise to six storeys, bursts forth into an array of delicately corbelled turrets each crowned with a simple conical roof. Magnificent plaster ceilings are a feature of the interior. The recollections which follow are by Sir Ewan Forbes, Baronet of Craigievar.

The National Trust for Scotland

Opening times:
May–September
Daily 13.30–17.30
Tel: (01339) 883635

Craigievar Castle was always a place of great excitement for me from my earliest childhood days. I was brought up to love and revere its fairy castle appearance as it shot straight up into the sky. I never felt that large castles spread out over many acres could possibly be castles. They were palaces or fortresses. A real castle was tall and thin and had a particular elegance of its own. That was our kind of castle.

It had the warmth of the red granite and a particular smell of its own which it still possesses today – the same as seventy years ago.

Its very artistic Scottish Baronial style allows the imagination to indulge itself. It is in fact a dream castle but of very solid structure. Its security was ensured by its one entrance – a massive yett. From high above I have often leaned out of my little bedroom window on moonlit nights and heard a tremendous tramping about and clanking of arms. But nothing could be seen.

The building of the castle was started by the Mortimers in the sixteenth century but when, about 1600, the lands and buildings were acquired by Willie the Merchant or Danzig Willie, my direct Forbes ancestor, the castle was completed by him. Between 1610 and 1626 he had it wonderfully·decorated with plastered designs on the ceilings. It was strongly erected as a fortress of the Reformed religion and a place where itinerant preachers were welcomed, given lodging and a place for meditation and prayer. Danzig Willie was a great upholder of the Reformation and prayer and his son, created a Baronet of Nova Scotia in 1630, was a very strong supporter of the Covenant.

He lead the Covenanting army against Montrose in Aberdeen and was twice taken prisoner. He held firm to his belief and predicted that if any of his descendants failed to support the Kirk of Scotland and the Covenant, the lands would surely be taken from them.

This truth was borne out when the tenth Baronet embraced the Roman Catholic religion. Nowadays the castle is safe forever under the care of the National Trust for Scotland.

Danzig Willie's elder brother was known as Patrick the Laird of Corse and later Bishop of Aberdeen. This was before the title of 'Bishop' was banished by the Kirk of Scotland on the advice of that great theologian Andrew Melville who realised the harm done by the privilege of the Bishops in the past. It was, therefore, decreed that all ministers should be equal.

During its entire history the castle has been continuously occupied by the Forbes and Forbes-Sempill family until the National Trust for Scotland were given the stewardship of the historic building in 1963.

The Footsteps on the Stairs

There have been many foolish and untrue ghost stories about Craigievar Castle, but there is no doubt that some experiences were true. As a family we were aware that after a large house party, such as used to be given when my sister was making her début in society, the unseen occupants of the castle were very annoyed and disturbed. A lot of tramping about and banging would be manifest all over the building.

I had such an experience one night about fifty years ago. My mother and I were resident in the castle alone. After our supper we were locked into the castle by the caretaker who took the key home with her. This was to allow her to get in to light the fire in the morning. Remember, there was only one door!

My mother slept on the fifth floor and, as she was beginning to feel tired, at nightfall I used to give her a hitch upstairs with my shoulder applied to her rear end. I then went down to the floor below. I was splashing in a warm bath when I heard footsteps very distinctly coming down the stairs. Thinking that she had mislaid her newspaper in the great hall I shouted: 'Hey ma, I'll get your paper for you.' No reply came back – just the persistent treading of feet. Wrapping the towel round me I jumped out of my bath and set off down the spiral staircase. The first thing that struck me was that there was no light as we had extinguished all the little paraffin lamps on the way up. Seizing my bathroom lamp I made my way down to the hall and the castle door.

Nobody was there to be seen. Up I climbed to my mother's bedroom and cross-questioned my dear Mama. She said that she had never been out of bed. There she was with her newspaper lying in front of her. Like the blowing out of the candle, the story ends here, in the eeriness of darkness.

144

thirlestane castle

Thirlestane Castle stands to the north-east of Lauder above the River Leader in the Borders region. It was built in approximately 1590 for the first Baron Maitland of Thirlestane on the site of the Old Fort of Lauder. The building was much extended in Restoration taste for the first Duke of Lauderdale. He built the jutting wings which flank the entrance on the west front, and to which in the nineteenth century, still further wings were added, completing the cross-bar of the 'T' shape.

The house is probably the most splendidly decorated in Scotland. Many rooms have rich plasterwork ceilings and contain fine furniture, paintings, and china.

The castle has been in the Maitland family to the present day, and is now owned by Captain the Honourable Gerald Maitland-Carew, grandson of the fifteenth Earl of Lauderdale; who wrote the following article.

Opening times:
Easter week, May, June and September
Mon, Wed, Thurs and Sun 14.00–16.30
July–August
Daily 14.00–16.30, except Sat
Tel: (01578) 722430; Fax: (01578) 722761

In the thirteenth century, Thirlestane was raised on solid rock above the silver windings of the River Leader to protect one of the main routes into Scotland against any invading English army. This 'Old Fort' has changed hands several times between the English and Scots and within its walls lies much history. To this day there is the old 'Oubliette Tower' where in the Dark Ages prisoners have been thrown to rot to death with little chance of escape.

In 1482 King James III with a Scottish army of some 50,000 soldiers camped around the Fort in preparation for stopping King Edward IV, with an English army, recovering Berwick. King James had surrounded himself with an odd bunch of friends and advisers of low birth. The nobles of Scotland had grown more and more restive and antagonistic towards these low-born counsellors. They took this opportunity to hold a conference in the Lauder Kirk conveniently situated near the Old Fort. Something, they agreed must be done to eliminate these men whose influence over the King was so offensive to them. At this point Cochrance, one of these queer friends, recently created Earl of Angus, entered the church with a message from the King. He was richly dressed and accompanied by a bodyguard of 300 men dressed in livery of white with black facings. He was immediately seized and a party of nobles sent to the King's pavilion to arrest the remaining favourites. They were hurried down to the wooden bridge over the Leader behind the Fort and there, in full view of the King, were hanged with tent ropes and horses' halters.

The Maitland family who had followed William the Conqueror from Normandy and settled in the Leader Valley had shown through generations unquestioned ability, giving prominent service to Scotland and being bound to their monarchs by personal affection. Between 1570 and 1590 the 'Old Fort' was transformed into his family home by Chancellor Maitland, Lord Chancellor to King James VI.

'Midside Maggie'
The Chancellor's grandson, the second Earl of Lauderdale, later created Duke of Lauderdale, has a famous Scottish story told about him. In 1651 the Earl of Lauderdale had a tenant, Thomas Hardie, on Midside Farm some four miles north of the old Castle, on the exposed

side of the Lammermuir Hills. He was married to Margaret, generally known as 'Maggie'. They were a hard-working young couple, but soon with a young family to feed, and a number of severe winters playing havoc with the flock which they herded on those exposed hillsides 1200 feet above sea-level, they found themselves in real poverty and distress. When the rent fell due, they had no money with which to pay it. Thomas was not prepared to ask the Earl for time to pay. His wife Maggie, however, was determined to save her home and family if she could. She made her way to Thirlestane Castle, gained an interview with the Earl and pled for time or mercy with such modest earnestness that he was moved to be generous. He would remit the rent that year but on one condition. Presumably she had made the substance of her plea the prolonged snow lying on the hills till late in the season for the last few years. She must prove the truth of her statement by bringing him a snowball from the farm in the month of June. The snow lies long in sheltered crannies of the Lammermuirs and she made sure it would do so on this occasion by packing it tightly in where the sun would not reach it. The Earl was as good as his word. When in June Maggie arrived at the castle with her snowball he accepted it as due payment of the rent.

By the following year the Earl was a prisoner, having been captured by Cromwell at the Battle of Worcester. He was kept first in Windsor Castle and then the Tower of London under sentence of death until the Restoration of Charles II. Between 1651 and 1659 the Hardies had prospered. They had saved money and Maggie decided to make the journey to London. Outside the Tower she sang 'Leader Haughs and Yarrow' a well-known Border folk-song. The Earl heard her and begged his gaoler to admit her, which he did. Once inside she handed over a bannock which she had baked. 'Come pree the bannock' she is supposed to have said, and when the Earl broke it, out tumbled the gold coins they had provided for his use, and with these coins he was able to much improve his living.

After the release of the Earl, he journeyed to Holland and on his return to Thirlestane he immediately sent for 'Midside Maggie' and presented her with a magnificent silver waist-chain as a personal reward for her loyalty and courage. Descendants of the Hardies still live in Lauder and the chain is now on display in the Museum of Antiquities in Edinburgh.

Thirlestane to this day is in the Maitland family and is proud to display to visitors its long history and show its lovely family treasures, and is a must to visitors in Scotland.

culzean castle

Culzean Castle overlooks the Firth of Clyde and was created by Robert Adam for the tenth Earl of Cassillis in the 1770s. Adam incorporated the original building – a stronghold of the Kennedy family – into the south side of his mansion. The interior has much fine plasterwork, an unusual oval staircase, and a round drawing-room.

The Castle and grounds were gifted to the National Trust for Scotland in 1945 by the fifth Marquess of Ailsa and the Kennedy family.

The grounds cover 565 acres and, in 1969, were declared Scotland's first Country Park. This is run in conjunction with the local authorities and has a wide range of facilities including a Ranger Service, deer park, information centre, and a comprehensive programme of countryside walks and lectures.

The account which follows was written by Mr Gordon Riddle, Principal, Culzean Country Park.

The National Trust for Scotland

Opening times:
April–October; other dates by appointment
Daily 10.30–17.30
Tel: (01655) 760274

The name Culzean is derived from Cuilean – literally, the place of the caves, and it is in the large caverns below the existing castle that we find the earliest evidence of occupation of the site. The stonework which fortifies the entrance to the main cave system reveals much older workmanship than that of Robert Adam and is in keeping with the tradition of cave-dwelling on the Ayrshire coastline.

Culzean's story can be neatly packaged into three sections and caves played a different role in each. The Kennedy family have been associated with the province of Carrick in South Ayrshire certainly since the end of the twelfth century and the early history of Culzean is bound up in the bloody conflict and struggle for supremacy between factions within the family.

The Kennedys can claim descent from the Earls of Carrick and kinship with the family of Robert the Bruce. John Kennedy is recorded as Steward of Carrick in 1367 and about the same time he acquired the lands of Cassillis. The power of the family was consolidated and confirmed when one of the family, James Kennedy of Dunure, married Princess Mary, daughter of King Robert III in 1405. Thereafter, with a comparatively weak central government under the Stuarts, partly dependent on the self-interest of the local magnates and the lairds, the family were able to establish a powerful grip on the area epitomised by the old verse:

> Twixt Wigtoun and the toun of Ayr
> Port Patrick and the Cruives of Cree,
> No man need think for to bide there,
> Unless he court wi' Kennedie.

To begin with the power of the Kennedys was not primarily centred on Culzean but rather at Dunure, four miles to the north, and on Cassillis, a little way inland to the north-west of the town of Maybole. Culzean is a natural fortress which could not be overlooked by a family seeking power in the area and David, great-grandson of James and Princess Mary became the first Earl of Cassillis and acquired the Lands of Culzean in 1505 from some obscure branch of the family.

The earliest paintings depict a bleak landscape and the lawless character of the area is well illustrated during the next century.

In 1575 Culzean first plays an important part in the family history. When the fourth Earl died, Culzean was in the hands of his younger brother Sir Thomas, and his eldest son and heir was still a very young child. Thomas, therefore, took over both the guardianship of the young Earl and the management of the estates. The first gave him the title of 'Tutor of Cassillis' by which he is generally known to this day.

About 1600, long-standing feuds within the family were rife and the Tutor pursued them as relentlessly as any. The main feud was between Gilbert Kennedy of Bargany and the Cassillis branch. In 1601 at a battle rashly undertaken by Bargany just south of Ayr, eighty of his men were confronted by 200 from Cassillis with predictable results. Bargany died in the fray and this marked the beginning of a rapid decline of this faction. Bargany's death was avenged five months later when the Tutor was murdered on the sands of Ayr and robbed of 2,000 pounds Scots.

This unsettled, violent period in Culzean's history is captured in S. R. Crocket's famous novel *The Grey Man* which follows the troubles through the adventures of young Tom Kennedy of Culzean. The story also has links with local caves, as one of the villains is the infamous local cannibal, Sawny Bean, who is reputed to have preyed upon unsuspecting travellers using the coastal route. He and his family, based in a cave in South Ayrshire were reported to have killed as many as a thousand people. He was eventually caught and executed.

Fiction aside, with the ascendancy of the Cassillis branch the first phase of the story comes to an end and though the Earls of Cassillis featured prominently in the struggle for ecclesiastical freedom which followed, the bloodshed of the previous centuries was over.

We take up the story again in 1759 when the power of the Kennedys had declined considerably and the eighth Earl died with no direct heir. The inheritance dispute went as far as the House of Lords till eventually Sir Thomas Kennedy, a direct descendant of the Tutor, was declared Earl.

Culzean then entered a decisive phase which was to alter its character profoundly.

Thomas was a soldier and a great traveller, spending many years in

England and on the Continent. He chose to stay at Culzean which became the principal seat of the family and embarked upon improving the land. It was a time of change in industry, agriculture, and communications and Thomas was keen to put into practice the new ideas which were eventually to transform this bleak heathland coastal area into the beautiful wooded estate we have today. Some improvements had already been made during the reign of Charles II when the glen in front of the Tower had been laid out as terraced gardens adorned with peach, apricot, cherry, and other fruit trees.

From an old drawing which has survived it seems that the house which Thomas lived in was a typical Scots tower house of the late sixteenth century and could possibly have been built by the Tutor. It stood where the central part of the present south façade now rises and indeed some of its masonry is incorporated in this part of Robert Adam's design. To the north, between the tower and top of the cliff lay the Barmkin, enclosing all the subsidiary domestic and utilitarian outbuildings which such an establishment required. Although his impact on the buildings was minimal he did bring Robert Adam to Culzean when he commissioned a design for a new Parish Kirk at Kirkoswald and the new Home Farm at Culzean.

When Sir Thomas died in 1775 his brother David succeeded him and, although he only lived at Culzean for short periods due to his career as an advocate in Edinburgh and a politician in London, he carried on where Thomas had finished. In 1777 he commissioned Robert Adam to convert the old dwelling-place into an elegant eighteenth-century mansion overlooking the terraced gardens to the south. One can only imagine the relish with which Adam tackled the contract to create the romantic Castle on the dramatic clifftop. The Castle was conceived less as a family home, more as a house for social entertainment. The old courtyard with the service buildings still remained after Adam's first phase but gradually he built round it, adding new service quarters in 1779 and the Round Drum Tower perched on the cliff edge. Ten years after he first began work here, Adam used the small, sunless courtyard to produce his magnificent Oval Staircase of which space and light are the very essence.

Adam was obviously very aware of the weight which he had placed on the clifftop and two support pillars were built in the caves just in case. Floor levels in the caves are much higher than would be expected and it is possible that Adam used this space as a convenient disposal point for the rubble.

In this short period of time a country seat was formed and the transformation continued through the early part of the nineteenth century. The most striking illustration of what must have been a momentous and exciting revolution in landscape, living conditions, and land use can be seen by comparing an old estate map of 1750 and the first Ordnance Survey Map of 1857. The old crofting system on an almost featureless heathland hillside was replaced by a well-afforested, enclosed landscape, laid out with Home Farm, Swan Pond, Walled Garden, and the numerous ancillary structures which make up the estate. Over 5,000,000 trees were purchased between 1800 and 1830 to provide the avenues, amenity areas, shelter, and production timber. The creation of a wooded environment must have completely altered the wildlife populations and the establishment of a strong song-bird population and rich floral communities were a beneficial by-product of the improvements. Even the spelling of Culzean changed. The more fashionable 'Culzean' replaced Cuilean though when and why are not recorded.

The stability which characterised Culzean from the middle of the nineteenth century onwards is epitomised by the life of Archibald, the third Marquis who succeeded to the title as a young man of twenty-two in 1870 and lived to the ripe old age of ninety. The title Marquis of Ailsa had been bestowed upon the twelfth Earl at the coronation of William IV in 1831.

Archibald had two main passions, the sea and Culzean. He was instrumental in developing much of the shipbuilding industry in the area, including the construction of a boathouse and harbour at Culzean. A photograph survives, and is displayed in the Castle, showing the *Beagle* being built on the slipway at Culzean. This ten-ton vessel, designed by the Fyfes of Fairlie, was launched in 1877 but subsequently run down and sunk in the Kyles of Bute in the same year. Much more famous, however, were his racing yachts – *Foxhound*, *Bloodhound* and *Sleuthhound*.

156

He was also a keen garden enthusiast and developed the Walled Garden and Happy Valley. In this age of the botanical explorer, many exotic plants like palms and rhododendrons were planted throughout Culzean. The West Wing was added to the Castle in 1879 and when the Maidens Dunure Light Railway line was opened in 1907 a station was built at Glenside for the use of the Marquis and his family. When he died his three elder sons became Marquis of Ailsa in turn.

The final phase in Culzean's story began with the bequest by the fifth Marquis of the Castle and its immediate policies to the National Trust for Scotland. This was a great challenge for the relatively new conservation organisation as the property was given without an endowment and Culzean embarked upon yet another change. Culzean rapidly became the Trust's most popular property gaining international recognition both as a tourist attraction and latterly as Scotland's first Country Park.

Visitors could now explore the 'upstairs' life of the Kennedy family, entering through the entrance hall with its impressive armoury made up of arms from the independent West Lowland Fencible Regiment in 1790. The imposing library, dining-room, and bedrooms surround Adam's outstanding Oval Staircase which cannot fail to draw a gasp of admiration. The Round Drawing Room with views over the Firth of Clyde is contrastingly beautiful. In many of the rooms research has revealed the original colour schemes and whenever possible these have been restored.

The top floor contains the National Guest Flat which was at the disposal of General Eisenhower during his lifetime as a token of the gratitude felt by the Scots for his war services. A modern presentation has been mounted to explain his role in the Second World War and his association with Culzean which he visited on four occasions, once as President of the U.S.A.

Restoration work has also been undertaken on the Castle exterior where constant exposure has resulted in severe erosion of the soft red sandstone. Each face of the Castle is being restored in turn thanks to grant-aid from the Historic Buildings Council. One beneficial side-effect has been the sight of skilled stonemasons at work.

The grounds were managed in line with normal estate practice with some provision for visitors but it was essentially low key, the emphasis quite rightly being on the Castle. This changed dramatically in 1969 when the grounds were declared Scotland's first Country Park and from an annual visitation of around 100,000 people, the number rose to 300,000 in a few years. It was pioneer days again as new techniques were developed to cope with the demanding management aim of maintaining the character of the Park while at the same time providing recreational opportunities and facilities for huge numbers of urban visitors.

Culzean once again rose to the challenge and soon gained both national and international recognition for the management of the property and the high quality of service offered. The unique partnership in management between the National Trust for Scotland and local and regional authorities with help from Government agencies such as the Countryside Commission for Scotland has survived the test of time.

A Ranger/Naturalist service was set up at the same time as the Country Park was formed to act as a link between the visitor and the Park. Adam's beautifully symmetrical Home Farm was converted into a superb modern visitor centre combining an information and interpretive section with shop, toilets, a large restaurant, and an administrative block. In the Park itself picnic sites were developed and pathway systems extended and, where appropriate, new structures such as hides, adventure playground, and a Deer Park added.

In line with the basic philosophy of Country Parks, a comprehensive programme of countryside walks and talks was developed by the Ranger Service to help people explore the different facets of Culzean and the Young Naturalists' Club formed in the earlier years has now matured into an exceptionally exciting concept. Over 300 children join the Club annually and become involved in all aspects of the day-to-day life of this piece of Scottish countryside. The caves come into our story for the last time as a venue for one of the most popular of the Ranger Walks.

The wealth of natural and historical resources available at Culzean makes it ideal for educational work and over 16,000 school pupils visit Culzean annually for some sort of outing linked to their classroom work. Not surprisingly, in 1984 Culzean won one of the Sandford Awards for an outstanding contribution to Heritage Education.

Today the far-sighted planning of the ninth and tenth Earls provides a vital recreational resource for both the local population and the tourist. The superb facilities provided by both the Castle and Country Park cater for a wide range of interests, from those who simply wish to explore an attractive area of countryside to the historian or family on holiday. I'm sure Robert Adam would have approved.

BRODICK CASTLE

Built of red sandstone, Brodick Castle occupies a commanding site in the Firth of Clyde, looking down on Brodick Bay, on the beautiful Isle of Arran. The ancient castle is a treasure-house set in glorious gardens. It was the home of the Dukes of Hamilton for nearly 600 years and then for one generation passed to the Duke of Montrose.

In 1958, following the death of the Duchess of Montrose, the castle and its associated chattels were accepted in lieu of estate duty by the Commissioners of Inland Revenue. In turn the National Trust for Scotland accepted future permanent responsibility at the request of the Treasury. The Lady Jean Fforde, daughter of the Duchess of Montrose, added the gift of 7,300 acres of mountain and glen.

The castle has exquisitely furnished apartments in which collections of silver, ivory, and porcelain are displayed. More functional, but no less interesting, is the recently restored Victorian kitchen complete with a water-driven roasting spit, still worked by the original mechanism. The old castle prison is also on view.

The castle is set in parkland which contains two superb gardens. The woodland garden has one of the finest rhododendron displays in Europe. A country park was established adjacent to the castle in 1980.

The account which follows was written by Lady Jean Fforde.

The National Trust for Scotland

Opening times:
Early April and October
Daily 13.00–17.00
Late April–September
As above, except Sun 12.00–17.00
Tel: (01770) 302202

The principal rooms at Brodick Castle were added to the old fortress when the eleventh Duke of Hamilton married Princess Marie of Baden. She, the daughter of Stephanie de Beauharnais (Napoleon's adopted daughter) had been brought up amid the social life of the Courts of Europe and ones sympathy goes to her when she married and found herself abandoned and alone in Brodick while her husband amused himself in the gambling-houses of London and Paris. She wrote sad letters of despair asking why he would not take her with him. She produced two sons and a daughter. Her daughter married Prince Albert of Monaco and then Prince Festetic of Hungary. Her younger son died in his thirties and the elder one (my grandfather), born in 1845, became the twelfth Duke of Hamilton. To occupy herself she sent for some workmen from her old home to build three summer-houses in the Bavarian style, octagonal in shape and lined from ceiling to floor in a mosaic of fir cones, the outside covered in a pattern of branches tacked to the structure. She laid out gravelled carriage roads through the woods to the summer-houses high on the hill above the castle. Two of these were later vandalised but one remains in the rock-garden.

As soon as the eleventh Duke died in 1863, Princess Marie left for the Hamilton's house in Paris where she remained for most of her life bringing up the young Duke until he went to Oxford. He, a rich young man in his twenties, then started to explore his possessions in Britain. These consisted of Hamilton Palace; in the town of Hamilton, together with the famous art collection there, left to his father by his great-grandfather, William Beckford; Easton Park in Suffolk; a London house; and the Isle of Arran. Like his father he took to gambling, as a result of which the palace was cleared of most of the art treasures which were auctioned at a famous four-day sale in 1882 to pay off his debts, but my grandmother rescued some of the collection for Brodick and Easton.

He, his wife and daughter, travelled from one property to the other, hiring a complete train and travelling with their servants, valuables, horses, dogs, and luggage. This mode of travel continued till 1923. On his death in 1895 he left all his possessions (with the exception of Hamilton Palace, which went with the title), in trust to his ten-year-old daughter and only child, Lady Mary Douglas Hamilton who married the sixth Duke of Montrose, my parents.

Sport was of prime importance to the family so Brodick was visited during the grouse shooting and the stalking season (August–October) and then she went south with the family for the hunting season. As both the Montroses and the Hamiltons had lost a fortune on the racecourses and at cards we were never taken near a racecourse and never allowed to play cards for money.

When my grandfather, the fifth Duke of Montrose died, my mother's trustees sold her London house and Easton Park and life became more orderly with six months at the Montrose family home – Buchanan Castle on Loch Lomond side – and six summer months at Brodick. Central heating was installed and electric light supplied by our own private generator, and Brodick became a home. The terraced banks below the castle had been covered by laurel; this was cleared, and my mother's passion for gardening began. Thorough in everything she did, it was not long before she met the famous plant-collectors of the day, took shares in their expeditions, and in return got a share of the plants they collected.

My father, who was deaf from boyhood, achieved an amazing amount when one realises he was fighting such a handicap. In his *My Ditty Book* he tells of his friendship with Dr John MacIntyre in whose house he met Lords Blythswood and Kelvin. 'On one occasion we obtained from America a very early type of kinematograph. It was a wooden box with a photographic lens and film reel inside it. There was a revolving shutter, which was rotated by turning a handle outside the box, after the style of a barrel organ. According to the pace at which the shutter was rotated, the film inside the box was exposed through the lens, and the photos were thus taken rapidly in sequence. Kelvin, Blythswood, MacIntyre and myself adapted this kinematograph to the fluorescent screen of the newly invented X-ray plant. One evening we got MacIntyre's parlour-maid to sit on a table, and move her leg up and down and sideways so that we could photograph the knee joint. This I believe to have been the first occasion in Great Britain when a joint on a living person was actually observed and photographed in motion.'

In 1899, under the chairmanship of the Lord Provost of Glasgow, Sir James Bell, my father held an open meeting to test public feeling about starting the Royal Naval Voluntary Reserve. It was not till 1902 the First Lord of the Admiralty brought the idea before the House of Commons and the R.N.V.R. was born, and the first officers were appointed. My father's commission was No. 1 and Sir Rupert Guinness No. 2, R.N.V.R. In his book my father says this was probably the maximum 'opus' of his life.

The interests of Scotland were of vital importance to him, and for this reason he changed his political party three times from Conservative to Liberal to Scottish National and back to Liberal once more, as he felt their doctrines would benefit Scotland most. He led the Scottish Trade Mission to Canada on the ship T.S.S. *Letitia* in 1932 to promote Scottish industries.

When the National Health Service started there was no aid allowed for the deaf. For many years he had pleaded in the House of Lords that help for the 400,000 registered deaf should be included in the National Health Bill but it was passed with the deaf excluded. It took many hours of debate before he got hearing aids and help with repairs allowed.

At the time he was fighting for this Bill he was Chairman of the Deaf Institute and as guest of honour at the Institute's annual dinner, Aneurin Bevan was invited. As my father received him, Bevan told him he had agreed to put a hearing aid on the National Health Service and he hoped my father would be satisfied. Father asked to see what kind of instrument he had in mind and was aghast to find it was an old-fashioned type with earphones and a separate box of batteries and another box with the microphone. Father refused to back Bevan and told him that he wanted the U.S.A. type which he was wearing. Only a plastic wire showed and a small plastic fitting in the ear, the other parts were inside his dress shirt. He promised to post it to the Minister when he returned to his Club which he did. Weeks later the Minister phoned to inquire where it was. Some secretary, when opening the Minister's mail, had found wire and batteries and thinking it was a bomb sent by the Stern Gang extremists, she called the police. Sadly his modern aid given to him by the American Deaf Institute and of which he was so proud, lay drowned in a tank at the police station.

He was Lord High Commissioner at the General Assembly of the Church of Scotland in 1942/43. My two brothers, on leave, both in the R.N.V.R. uniform and my father in his Commodore R.N.V.R. uniform made me very proud as they stood on the lawns of Holyrood Palace for the official photograph.

After the war we went to different ends of the earth. Angus, the present Duke of Montrose, returned to his home in Zimbabwe; Ronald to Jamaica; I married and lived in Palestine then Sierra Leone, followed by Zambia. My sister Mary lived with her family in Surrey.

When we meet the conversation returns to those happy days in Brodick Castle, the house full of friends and many of our foreign relations. The Monaco family came each summer for a long visit which I looked forward to, as Princess Antoinette is exactly my age, and Prince Rainier two years younger. The Markgraff of Baden was my idol, because he always stood up for me and took me fishing and rabbit-shooting. Harry Lauder stayed on two occasions and performed in the village hall for some of my mother's fund-raising efforts. Helen Keller, the famed blind, deaf, and dumb lady visited and through her interpreter could hold a conversation. She had to run her hands over people's faces and bodies to get the feel of what they looked like. My father's kilt needed some explanation and caused a lot of laughter!

Both my mother and my father had a secretary and their work kept both women in full time employment.

My mother worked untiringly for the island and started the Women's Rural Institute, the meetings of which had to be held on the nights of the full moon to give the farmers' wives the chance of some light to walk many miles from their homes to the village halls. The moon seldom shows here as we get seventy-five inches of rain a year! She instigated the War Memorial Hospital as there was no hospital before, and she felt it better to spend money on this living reminder of our dead rather than for each village to spend money on elaborate memorials. The Music Festival, now a three-day affair, was close to her heart as she had studied music abroad and played the violin well. When she started this it met with great enthusiasm as did the Drama

Festival. For many years she had entries of up to twenty one-act plays.

I am often asked if, as a child, I realised how privileged I was. Of course not – it was the only life I knew, and I envied the village children their freedom to run wild, stay out late at night, and eat ice-creams as they walked along the village street. Eating snacks in public was forbidden by Nanny – very 'naughty'. Did I miss a great deal being brought up by a Nanny? I don't think so, because when taken to the drawing-room to play after tea I had the full and undivided attention of my mother and often of my father. Spending Sunday afternoon with them was like a special holiday. I was taken down to the drawing-room but had to go up to the nursery myself. The hall and stairway was panelled from top to bottom with stuffed stags' heads with glass eyes which caught the light. I would scamper as fast as I could, long fair hair flying out from my head, white socks and red shoes that hardly touched the ground. Obviously, grown-ups did not realise the panic those beastly heads caused me.

I suppose the young would find our life constricting and formal but it was the only way of life we knew and we conformed. Meals were punctual and we were severely reprimanded if we were late. Dinner at 8 p.m. was a full-dress affair, dinner-jackets for the men and long dresses and beautiful jewellery for the ladies; the dinner-table decorated with fine silver or silver-gilt, the polishing of which was the pride of Mr Allan the butler. He started as a boot boy to my grandmother, and served four generations. As a child I was afraid of him. If I came in late from our boat or the tennis court he would be standing guard outside his pantry, 'Hurry up there, who do you think you are, late again. I'm not having my men [the footmen] kept late just for you, get on and be quick.' I rushed to my room, flung on my clothes, and dashed panting to the drawing-room where everyone else was assembled. The double doors into the library which led to the dining-room would open and with great dignity Mr Allan would announce, 'Dinner is served Your Grace.' 'It's late,' my mother would retort. 'An unavoidable delay Your Grace,' and so I was saved again.

Through my childhood I had been threatened that the 'grey lady' would catch me. She haunted the back quarters of the house, the oldest parts. She was dressed in grey with a large white collar of Cromwellian times but we never saw her until just before my mother's death. Mother was ill and employed a housekeeper/companion. She was a medium and believed in controlled handwriting. While she was in the castle four people saw the grey lady walking along the back passage or standing watching them doing their housework. Through the housekeeper's controlled writing she was told the grey lady had been in the household when Cromwell's garrison was stationed there and conceived a baby by one of the officers. She was turned out of the castle and took her life at the Old Quay below the castle. Also a man in a green velvet coat and light-coloured breeches has been seen sitting reading in the library.

The tradition of a white deer seen on the hill when the head of the resident family dies seems real. There was a silver-grey hind seen just before my father died. A pure white calf was born four months after my mother died and another was born before my brother, Lord Ronald, died. I am sure scientists could explain it, but nevertheless it has appeared three times.

Perhaps now we have lost the castle and it is no longer our home, there will be no more white deer on the hill.

Fyvie castle

This impressive fortified castle stands in wooded parkland, close to the village of Fyvie in the Grampian region. Its great façade has been likened to that of a French château, although Fyvie is the result of the combined inventions of five families who were to own the castle in succession (the Prestons, the Meldrums, the Setons, the Gordons, and the Leiths). Each family has a tower or wing named after it.

It is thought that the oldest part of the castle still to stand was built about 1400 by Sir Harry Preston. This is known as the Preston Tower.

Fyvie Castle is now in the care of the National Trust for Scotland, and will open to the public for the first time in 1986. It is a castle steeped in history and strange tales, some of which have been related here by Mr Christopher Hartley, Assistant Curator, National Trust for Scotland.

The National Trust for Scotland

Opening times:
Easter week, May–September
Daily 13.00–17.30
June–August
Daily 11.00–18.00
Early – late October
Sat and Sun 13.30–17.30
Tel: (01651) 891266

The five towers of Fyvie enshrine five centuries of Scotland's turbulent history. Its skyline bristles with bartizans. Atop of every turret balance three-foot-high stone statues of warriors marshalled towards every quarter of the compass. Only the figure of Andrew Lammie, the Laird of Fyvie's trumpeter, who forever sounds his silent horn from the roof-top of the Preston Tower towards the Mill of Tifty, where dwelt the beautiful miller's daughter whose love for the trumpeter was cruelly broken by her ambitious family, heralds a note of tragic romance. Gun loops keep silent watch. Machicolations await to welcome assailants with stones, pitch, and molten lead. The atmosphere is atavistic – or so it appears, for this embattled air is bombast; the sham display and architectural exuberance of an age already wise to the relentless force of gunpowder.

But Fyvie Castle's origins are earlier and darker than this. Long before the castle's oldest surviving tower was raised the land was a royal hunting forest with a fortlaise. The name means 'Deer Hill' in Gaelic. In the thirteenth century William the Lion and Alexander III were resident here during the peripatetic wanderings of the Court. The Hammer of the Scots, Edward I of England, held court at Fyvie on Sunday 22 July 1296 during his punitive expedition through Scotland. King Robert the Bruce dispensed justice in the beech woods of Fyvie. These royal visitors presaged the visits of other crowned heads to Fyvie in later centuries.

Fyvie ceased to be a Crown property after the Battle of Otterburn in 1388, immortalised in the famous 'Ballad of Chevy Chase', when the castle was granted to Sir James Lindsay, Earl of Crawford, as 'prize-money' for taking Sir Ralph Percy as prisoner-of-war. This episode is recorded in a plaster relief above the entrance hall fireplace. The present baronet of Fyvie, Sir Andrew Forbes-Leith, points it out to visitors with the succinct remark, 'That's the Lindsays clobbering the Percys.' Lady Lindsay found herself besieged at Fyvie by her nephew, Robert Keith. Nothing daunted, the indomitable lady ordered all the pewter chargers, plates, and chamber-pots to be melted down and poured on the heads of her upstart nephew and his cronies.

The estate passed from the Lindsays to the Preston family by marriage. The Prestons built the earliest part of the castle still to

171

stand and known as the Preston Tower. All four families who were to own the castle in succession to the Prestons were to follow their example and build their towers. Thus there followed the Meldrum Tower, the Seton Tower, the Gordon Tower, and the Leith Tower. But just as the story of Fyvie becomes tangible stone and mortar so the mists of ancient legend begin to envelop Fyvie's massy walls.

The Curse of the 'Three Weeping Stones'

This tale has been told in Aberdeenshire for many a day, and has lost nothing in the telling. It is a tale fit for a winter's night to be recounted by the light of a log fire which draws unexpected shadows from darkened corners. So I first heard it when I came to work in Scotland eight years ago and was staying with the owner of Castle Fraser, not a dozen miles from the legendary and secret Castle of Fyvie.

Several versions of the story exist. One recounts a promised visit to be made to the castle by the portentous seer, Tammas the Rhymer, 'a prophet of gloomy foreboding, who invariably . . . uttered his predictions with a studied ambiguity' as Mrs Stirling astutely writes in her picturesque history *Fyvie Castle, its lairds and their times*. Not wanting to upset the touchy visitor, the castle gates were set open in anticipation and welcome. For seven years and a day they stood expectantly 'wall wide' but as the seer approached, a freak storm blew up, tearing leaves from the trees and slamming shut the great gates in the face of the outraged poet, who stood at the centre of this vortex 'where there was not wind enough to shake the hair of his beard.' With predictable inevitability Tammas pronounced a curse upon the lands and castle one version of which runs:

> Fyvyn's riggs and towers,
> Hapless shall your mesdames be,
> When ye shall hae within your methes,
> Frae harryit kirk lands, stanes three;
> Ane in the oldest tower,
> Ane in my ladie's bower,
> And ane below the water-yett,
> And it ye shall never get.

The popular interpretation of this enigmatic utterance is the necessary identification of the three stones, which are thought to be old boundary markers ('methes' means boundaries) between the kirk and secular lands of Fyvie. One is built into the 'oldest tower' and one is in 'my ladie's bower' and thought to be the stone recorded earlier this century in the Charter room and which was kept in a wooden bowl. At unpredictable intervals it would fill the bowl with moisture. The last lies somewhere on the bed of the River Ythan that runs through the policies and 'this ye will never get'.

What was the implication of so unfulfillable a portent? None is stated, but it is popularly believed that the curse of the Weeping Stones is attached to whichever family owns the property and that the heir will never inherit – a situation uncannily demonstrable in the course of Fyvie's fluctuating fortunes.

The Secret Chamber

Fyvie has other and more traditional manifestations. Like Glamis it has a secret room. Once house guests placed towels at every window of the castle under the knowledgeable guidance of a puzzled housekeeper only to find five windows unmarked. Three of these were later accounted for, but two remained unexplained. Indeed a secret chamber lies beneath the Charter room to which no access exists and any attempt to open it up invokes another Fyvie curse which causes death to the Laird and blindness to his wife. General Gordon once attempted to discover the secret room's rumoured treasure but failed, dying soon after. From that time his wife, a one-time domestic in the castle by whom he had a natural son and whom he later married, thus legitimizing the offspring of that illicit union under the benign ruling of Scottish law, began to be afflicted by a blindness that became total and with which she went to her grave.

Later Sir Maurice Duff-Gordon reopened investigations. But before reluctant workmen could accomplish anything of significance he suffered a fall in the drawing-room and broke his leg. He ordered the work to stop before anything worse happened but his wife began to suffer from the onset of an eye irritation which was to worry her for the rest of her life.

173

The Green Lady of Fyvie

More potent still is the spectre of the Green Lady of Fyvie. Who was she? Accounts are confusing and confused. One claims that one of the Ladies Dunfermline was locked in a small room at the top of the great wheel stair built by Alexander Seton, first Earl of Dunfermline and up which the baby Charles Stuart, later King Charles I, took some of his earliest steps. For what forgotten crime she was incarcerated is not disclosed. Here she was held by guards by whom all who attempted her rescue were slaughtered before her eyes and thrown out of a window close by. Her brain was turned and the hapless lady was transfered to the room later to be known as the Gordon bedroom and there remained shut up until her death by starvation, as some say. The small panelled room at the top of the great stair became known as the 'murder room' and was supposed to have irremovable bloodstains on the floor. And who knows but that they may be there still hidden under the blue carpet?

Others equate the Green Lady with Dame Lilias Drummond, wife of the first Earl of Dunfermline, who bore her husband five daughters and never the longed-for heir. He fell in love with bonny Grizel Leslie, a daughter of the House of Leslie whose home, Leslie Castle, lies only twenty miles from Fyvie. Suddenly Grizel's step-aunt, Dame Lilias, died mysteriously and six months later the Earl married the young and beautiful Grizel. On the wedding night when Dame Lilias was supplanted by the younger and fairer rival the happy couple heard heavy sighs outside their chamber window. In the morning, deeply cut into the window-sill in characters nearly three inches high and written from without was found the name of the dead wife:

D LILIAS DRUMMOND

And there it is to this day.

Some say the coming of the Green Lady bodes evil to the reigning family at Fyvie. But one peculiarity has been attributed to her. It is said she desires that each Laird of Fyvie who breathes his last within the castle shall expire in the room where she herself suffered and died; and there, too, at times, though invisible, she makes her presence known by a wan, mysterious light. In later years the belief prevailed, quite unaccountably, that the Green Lady was visible only to one of Gordon blood. The following tale is told in illustration:

A wife of one of the Deputy-Sheriffs of Aberdeen came to stay and brought her maid called Thompson. This maid innocently reported that she had seen a lovely woman in a green satin dress going up the great staircase at midnight. When this was reported at the breakfast table, everyone present disclaimed being the owner of the green dress, till someone remarked, 'Surely it must have been the Green Lady. But she never appears except to a Gordon.' The lady from Aberdeen looked startled. 'Oh,' she replied, 'I always call my maid "Thompson" whoever she may be. The woman's name *is* Gordon!'

In 1879, when his elder brother Cosmo lay ill in the south, Alick Gordon was coming along the passage from the Gordon bedroom to the great stair one early December afternoon when he saw before him the Green Lady, faintly iridescent in the waning light. She dropped him a low curtsey and drifted away. He rushed, shaken, to the room where his wife sat sewing. 'I have just seen the Green Lady and she has saluted me as head of the family. My brother Cosmo will die.' On the 8 December the mournful news of Cosmo's death was brought to Fyvie.

Following Captain Alick Gordon's death the property passed to his cousin Maurice Duff-Gordon. Janet, his sister, lived in Italy with her husband Henry Ross. She visited her brother, the new Laird of Fyvie in 1884 and has left this account: 'During the last illness of my cousin, Captain Gordon, he was moved from the Gordon bedroom, the walls of which were hung with the Gordon tartan, into one near by; partly because it was more cheerful, partly because of the tradition that every Laird who died at Fyvie must die in the Gordon room. Mrs Gordon was called away for a few minutes, and on returning, to her terror, found bed and room empty. She called, servants came running, and the Laird was found in a fainting condition in the fateful room. When he recovered consciousness he told his wife that as she left the room the Green Lady glided in and beckoned to him. He felt compelled to obey and followed her to the Gordon bedroom.' He died shortly afterwards on the steps of his bank in Aberdeen where he had gone to sign before his banker and his lawyer the papers that would disinherit his profligate cousin and heir, Maurice Duff-Gordon, who thus succeeded to the estate by the skin of his teeth. But Captain Gordon's instinct was right. By 1885 the estate was on the market.

Not far away at Blackford lived Margaret Forbes who had married Admiral Leith, a younger son of General Alexander Leith-Hay of Leith Hall. In 1847 they had a son whom they christened Alexander Forbes-Leith. The story is told that one day the six-year-old Alexander set off, unknown to his parents, to walk all the way to Fyvie, the castle of which he had no doubt been told tales and of his blood connection with it through the Prestons. Passing through the awesome Den of Fyvie, the young boy approached the four-towered castle and, stretching up, managed to tug at the bell-pull. A servant opened the door and, wondering, inquired of the boy what his business was. 'I have come to see Fyvie,' was the answer; 'I mean to have it some day'.

Admiral Leith died when Alexander was eight, and his widow took her four children to live in Berlin, where living was comparatively cheap. Alexander was educated in Germany and Gosport. He entered the Navy in 1860. It was while HMS *Zealous* was laid up in San Francisco that he met Marie-Louise January, a considerable heiress. His subsequent career was meteoric. He became a tycoon in the American steel industry.

News was brought to him that Sir Maurice Duff-Gordon, having run into financial difficulties, was selling up. In 1889 Alexander Forbes-Leith bought the castle that he had visited as a boy of six. He had realised his childhood dream and was the Laird of Fyvie.

Fyvie as we see it today is the result of his love and energy in its embellishment. It is a *tour de force* and a fragile reminder of a brilliant, brittle era, now vanished beyond recall, obliterated by the sound of the guns across the trenches of the Great War.

During this conflict many country houses were required to play their part in the war effort. The present Laird told me that his great-grandfather, Lord Leith of Fyvie as Alexander was to become, said good-bye to his wife and drove into Aberdeen one day during the war to conduct some business. On his return late that afternoon he found a military hospital established in his home. Shortly after his

176

departure Lady Leith had received a telegram from the War Office informing her that Fyvie Castle was to be requisitioned and that the first patients would be arriving that afternoon. All was a flurry of activity as priceless paintings and furniture were rushed into a hastily contrived store in the drawing-room and gallery at the top of the Gordon Tower and army beds were being unloaded from a convoy of lorries at the front door below. By the time Lord Leith returned home that evening a calm and efficient hospital was running smoothly.

The Canadian Captain

A strange sequel rose out of Fyvie's war work. A Canadian Captain who had been one of the patients at Fyvie was invited back during his convalescence. He was a hard-headed, practical mining engineer who had no belief in the supernatural. He was assigned to the Gordon dressing-room. It was remarked afterwards how, on the first night he was full of talk and enjoyment; the second night he looked preoccupied; the third he was noticeably silent; and subsequently during the remainder of his visit, he seemed obviously ill at ease.

This is his story:

'If anyone had told me before I came here that there were such things as ghosts or anything supernatural, I should have looked upon that man as an arrant fool. Yet I can only tell you what happened to me here. The first night, tired with my journey, I fell into a heavy sleep. Some hours later I awoke with a sudden start, and a conviction that someone was in my room. The room was lit up, but there was no one to be seen; and finding that I had, as I thought, left the electric light on, I got out of bed to turn it off. But, so doing, to my amazement, I found that I turned it on! I extinguished it once more, but the light remained. The room was illuminated from some other source, and as I watched, the light got brighter. It was like little flames playing round the pictures, and I could see the colours quite distinctly. Since then, the same thing has happened every night. I fall asleep tired out, and awake to the same experience. All the time I feel there is something in the room but I can see no one, only this mysterious light which gets brighter as time goes on! I simply daren't go to bed.'

177

Sitting up into the early hours and recounting this experience to a fellow guest, who was in fact the husband of the Mrs Stirling already referred to, he and his companion finally turned in. Mr Stirling had a strange dream that the Captain had come to him in alarm but that he was unable to rouse himself and go to the frightened man's assistance. In the morning when he came down to breakfast, the Canadian was gone. Noting the absence of the visitor, Lord Leith happened to comment with some surprise on his hurried departure, and was told the cause. He was deeply interested. 'I know that does happen in that room,' he said, 'but I did not think anyone who did not belong to the Laird's family would ever see it. My brother saw it, and refused to sleep there again; and I myself have seen it; still more I have had the matter investigated scientifically, but so far no explanation has ever been suggested.'

Lord Leith was to face tragedy in his own family. His only son, Percy Forbes-Leith was to die, aged nineteen, of enteric fever contracted while fighting in the Boer War. The estate passed to his only daughter, Ethel Louise, and from her to her second son, Sir Ian. Of his two boys, the eldest was killed in the Malayan campaign and the estate was inherited by his second son, Sir Andrew Forbes-Leith, following the death of Arthur Forbes-Leith in the First World War. Sir Andrew recalls, with a smile, a blood-curdling scream emitted by his Governess in the schoolroom next to the old library at Fyvie. But this was no response to the supernatural but a result of Sir Andrew setting loose a mouse!

In 1984 Sir Andrew sold the castle and policies to the National Trust for Scotland. On 1 November I rang the great bell in the castle courtyard and was admitted to this secretive house, seen by so few in recent years, and the castle quietly entered upon another chapter in its long and eventful history. Will its legendary atmosphere, dismissed with a sceptical wave of his hand by Sir Andrew, endure? Is not all this speculation and story-telling the fruit of an age lit by guttering candles, of tapestries set mysteriously in motion by chronic draughts, and of weird noises caused by faulty flues? Will the stuffed American bison head, the elk head, or stuffed polar bear strike terror in the heart of a casual visitor on a late September afternoon? Will the standing suits of armour raise a spectral halberd in salute as a crocodile of schoolchildren file past the wonders of Fyvie, historical questionnaires in hand, on their way to the tea-room? Will the Green Lady ever be seen again drifting down the wide treads of the great wheel stair up which the Gordons rode their horses for a wager? Perhaps not . . . and yet?